THE
BUTCHER'S
TALE

THE
BUTCHER'S
TALE

NICHOLAS WALLS

This is a work of fiction. Names, characters, businesses, places, events, locales, and incidents are either the products of the author's imagination or used in a fictitious manner. Any resemblance to actual persons, living or dead, or actual events is purely coincidental.

The Butcher's Tale

Cover design by Anca Gabriela of BRoseDesignZ.
Interior design by Francis Nguyen.
Edited by Hanna Bauman of Between the Lines Editorial.

ISBN-13 978-1-7328016-0-8

Acknowledgements

It takes a village to raise an idiot, which explains why I'm still here. To compile a full list would take more pen and ink than the story itself. So, thank you everyone. You know who you are.

CHAPTER 1:
VICARIOUS REALITY

JOHNNY C. VID, the man, the myth, the legend, looked down the sloping peak with a confident sneer. Stretched out below, his millions of cheering fans seemed like little ants, but even from his lofty height Johnny heard their roaring adulation. Praising him. Worshipping him.

As well they should. Beneath him lay Death Peak, an artificial mountain and death trap all in one. Beyond that, a full mile of assorted spikes, spinning blades, and firepits, which he, Johnny C. Vid, would jump! Who else would dare such a monumental stunt? Who else but the man himself, El Vid!

Heart pounding in his ears, Johnny ran one last check on his veloci-sled, the advanced snowmobile perched like a silver bullet on the slope. The egg

shaped pod was little more than a smooth plas-
steel shell around an oversized engine but it was the
fastest thing on hover rails. The crackling array of
anti-grav discs beneath it made it the perfect vessel to carry Johnny through his death-defying stunt.
*Inertial dampers, check. Engine humming loud enough to
rattle my teeth. Grav fields are go.* Tension coiled in his
stomach, a viper ready to pounce.

He was ready.

The instant Johnny released the throttle, a wall
of force hit him like the hand of an angry god. Eyes
blurring with tears, it took all of his effort to hold
the rocket on course, plummeting down the mountain towards the ramp. Then, he was soaring through
the air like a chrome-plated angel.

Johnny reveled in the sensation. Free. Untouchable. Invincible. When he reached to ignite the secondary burners, to launch him to the other end, he
hit a snag. There was nothing there. His hand hit air.
Frantic, the daredevil looked down to see a patch of
grey nothing, fuzzy static where advanced instruments should be. Worse...it seemed to be spreading,
a burning hole in reality swallowing Johnny whole.

As the crackling miasma rushed over his eyes,
Johnny woke up. He winced as a buzzing noise
drilled into his brain from both ears. Someone kept
shouting at him again and again and again.

"Time up! Time up! Time up!" Unsteadily pushing off the polished steel table he'd been slouching against, Johnny barely registered disgust at the puddle of drool left behind. With a soft hiss the cable threading Johnny to the wall plug ejected, whizzing back into the socket beneath his ear fast enough to jerk his head back. Rubbing at the tender flesh around the cybernetic dataport, Johnny glared balefully at the outlet.

The soft embrace of VR, Vicarious Reality, faded away, the absence of the recorded memories leaving him cold and aware of the real world's tender mercies. Johnny shuddered as it all settled back on him. He wasn't a daredevil stuntman and this wasn't a stunt course in a faraway land. He was Johnny C. Vid, washed up shock-jock and strung-out junkie living in the less than gleaming metropolis of the Heap. He was currently slouched over in Happy Daze, a delightful little dive bar and VR joint that offered about every distraction you could want, for a bit of credit. About as far from the wealth and fame of reporting the news in front of countless viewers on the Net as one could possibly fall.

Reality bites.

Scratching anxiously at the dataport on his neck, Johnny turned to the glowing screen at the back of Daze. On it, larger than life, Obadiah Bidwell reported yet another grisly murder. Bidwell was a shock-jock, like Johnny used to be, and one that took obscene relish in recounting the chilling details. His ivory toothed grin, flashing brightly against obsidian dark skin, robbed the tragic news report of any sympathy, reducing it to crude spectacle and bloody theatre.

Not that it mattered.

None of the other junkies or imbibers in Happy Daze so much as looked up as gore splattered pictures trawled across the wall-sized screen. Wouldn't have made any difference even if they weren't lost chasing someone else's dreams. This was the Heap. No one cared. Just one more life snuffed out before breakfast.

Johnny might have cared once. Hell, he might even have covered the thing.

Johnny had been a paler copy of Bidwell, a newscaster chasing wars and murders for a blurb on the primetime vid-cast. But that was a lifetime ago. Now, he had more in common with burnouts, addicts, and junkies in the little dive bar than he did with the grinning shock-jock and his ten-thousand-credit suit.

Wiping dried drool from his mouth and hugging his stained trench coat tight, Johnny C. Vid smothered any thoughts of the past and wandered out into the streets to find his next hit.

He walked amidst flickering neon streetlights, their shadows falling like a shroud over the garbage and castoffs of the city, human and otherwise. Johnny shuffled past derelicts sitting on thrones of trash, the final remnants of their lives and others, piles gathered for warmth, protection, or because they had nothing else. Hard-eyed gangers watched him pass, fiercely guarding their little corner of urban hell. Burnouts raged at invisible demons, gibbering their enlightenment, their incomprehensible Cassandra Truths, to an uncaring audience. Broken concrete and hyper-steel struts propped up crumbling buildings, but nothing supported the broken hopes, dreams, and bodies of the people living here.

Johnny's eyes jerked skyward as another freighter roared through sulfurous clouds overhead. The bulky vessel barely slowed, dumping its cargo into the growing mounds of junk that gave the Heap its name before rising again through the halo of smog that encircled the urban sprawl. Miles and mountains of the unwanted remains of an interstellar civilization's industry. Racks of crushed cars, enough broken parts to build a factory or ten, and outdated smelters, sifters, ovens, engines, and more besides. Small or large, commercial or industrial, anything the great and good no longer wanted all fell onto the Heap. One mammoth shitpile monument to an empire's greatness.

Johnny shook his head and had to fight down the nausea that came with it. The reluctant reality attendant couldn't remember the last time he ate and his whole body ached.

Still, a bit of VR will take care of that little problem.

Johnny hurried home, knuckles clenched white on his soiled coat.

≈

"Home" was a dilapidated flophouse shared by an ever shifting crew of vagrants. The castoffs stuck together, bound by necessity and mutual mistrust.

Johnny didn't know the names of half of them. Even better, they didn't know his.

What Johnny did know was the little wizened figure talking animatedly to one of his "roommates," ruined teeth bared in a broad, unfriendly smile. His black and yellow gap tooth grin was noteworthy enough that it gave the stunted creature his street name: Smiler. Johnny's latest purveyor of Vicarious Reality. Only a pusher would wear a suit that shade of purple in the Heap. It acted as a beacon amongst the bare concrete and drywall.

"Johnny!" The goblin turned to smile at him, all stains and rot and tarnished chrome. "What can I do for you?"

"Hey, Smiler. Wondering if you got any of the goods?" Johnny would've cringed at the desperation in his voice if his need wasn't riding him so hard.

It didn't seem possible, but somehow the stunted creature's grin widened further. "I have just the thing." He reached into his obnoxiously colored suit and pulled out a little black box, dotted with multi-hued jacks. Blue, yellow, pink, and more besides, each promising a thousand different sensations and memories. A thousand escapes from the mundane world and its bloodshed and suffering.

Johnny's mouth watered just looking at it.

Smiler arched an eyebrow, enjoying his customer's squirming. "You know I always got you, Johnny. Good stuff. Primo. Only cost you twice my usual rate."

Damn. No wonder the bastard's smiling. It's fucking criminal. I should bargain and haggle this little shit down. I should...but I need it. Johnny paused, his craving warring with his pride. *Just this once.*

"Sure, sure, I know you're good for it. And you know I'm good for it. But for that price, I wanna make sure it's worth it. Let me sample the VR before I lay down the creds."

The pusher grinned like the Cheshire Cat, a cruel feline amused by a mouse's struggling. "Normally I wouldn't..." A politician couldn't lie so well. "But for one of my best customers..." Gangly fingers plucked out a colored line and held it out with all the reverence and ritual of communion.

Johnny snatched the little jack from Smiler like a starving man grabbing for a steak.

Wire slotted behind the ear. Neural feed singing over the cords. Through the bone to the spine, round to the brain. Straight hit on the joy buzzer. Direct line to nirvana. But rather than being carried away to a lovely new world, one free of the hurt and pain of mundane reality, Johnny crashed into a scathing wall of feedback. Static nails on his brain. Muffled echoes of another life wrapped in shattered emotional glass.

Johnny snapped the cable free with a curse. "What the hell are you trying to peddle here, Smiler?" He glared at the little creature who didn't even have the grace to look sheepish.

"What can I say, Johnny? Must have been wired wrong when they recorded it."

The hard-up junkie rubbed anxiously at his port, trying to scratch phantom pains away. The little shit's story checked out, at first whiff. *Slagging thing could be amateur work, blind-dumb recording by the person doing the living.*

Johnny knew all about the theoretical of VR. Knew all about the practical, too. For Vicarious Reality to work, a person had to live it. Another life, bottled, shipped, and free to taste. Johnny had been a cop, special ops, a lawyer, and even a skin-flick star. But the VR didn't always take.

Get it wrong, input to output, crossed wires and all you got was brain static. Do it wrong hard enough, often enough, you could slag some pretty vital bits of grey matter.

Damn if I didn't get a taste of something potent under all that static. Buried deep in the static, but real strong. One of the Primals; fear, anger, lust. The good shit.

Johnny wanted it. He wanted it more than he'd ever wanted anything in his life. In the dull burnt-out remnants of Johnny's soul, strong emotions blazed like bright beacons in the night. They colored the deep grey cloud that was his sad existence. It let him taste life without waking the old pains a lifetime of chasing horrors as a shock-jock left him. Let him actually live without waking ancient demons and seeing the glassy dead eyes that haunted his dreams and the tiny, little, sheet covered bodies.

So yeah, Johnny wanted it. And if Johnny let any of that hunger slip out, Smiler would own him.

Time to see if that time as Johnny the Champion Stud-Poker player is gonna come in handy.

"Even if it wasn't broken, it wasn't half as good as you played it up to be." Sneering, Johnny leaned in on the pusher, despite his protesting nose. "Where did you dig up that amateur hour crap up anyway?"

Smiler never lost his namesake grin. "Feeling entrepreneurial, eh Johnny boy? I can respect that."

The pusher took his junkie buddy's arm and looked around, suspicious of eavesdroppers. As if any of the deadheads could muster the attention for it. Rule One in the Heap: you mind your own business and look after yourself. "Truth is, all my suppliers been nervous lately, drying up on me. So I found this little gem out in the Boneyard. Primo scrap, primo finds." Again, that grin with more missing teeth than not.

The Boneyard. Shit. Johnny felt his stomach drop at mention of the dead zone. Nobody was ever stupid enough to call the Heap safe but the Boneyard's rep spooked even the locals. A sprawling stretch of ruins and junk anyone with half a brain avoided. Any sane man wouldn't even have considered going. Even if they had, common sense and survival instinct would have kicked in and made them forget the whole affair.

But when a junkie needs a hit, little things like sanity and sense take a backseat.

"Yeah? Thanks for the tip, squib." Johnny shouldered past the riotously clad pusher, driven by need and the last dregs of his pride.

≈

The sick cocktail of pride and need rode Johnny like a race pony as he hopped off the last tram-line and passed beyond the nominal borders of the Heap, past the pushers and pimps, past the gang territories and their endless petty wars, past the lights almost bright enough to drown out the broken hearts and shattered dreams. Johnny stepped past the boundaries of even that urban hell into something darker, that even the coldest eyed street-dwellers stayed well away from.

Neon advertisements gave way to flickering street lamps and even they fell away until only the utility-lights of the streets and the roadway remained, leaving Johnny to be swallowed up by muted night as he passed beyond the edges of the Heap and into the Boneyard.

The shock-jock's throat went dry as he caught his first glimpse of the towering piles of detritus looming in the dark, distant lights picking out glints of metal and matte plastics, discards pressed into several stories of amalgamated crap. Johnny paused, looking of at the shadowed peaks.

Fuck, do I really need to do this? Johnny hands clenched into fists when he thought of Smilers smug grin but more than that, his mouth watered when he thought of the static laced sample the garish coated pushed gave him. Just a taste, but it was enough. *Yes.*

Choking down the sick feeling in his guts Johnny pushed onward, sliding between the rows of trash like a ghost.

Sometime later, after what felt like an eternity of sifting through broken toys, appliances, and shards too mangled to put a name on, a new emotion rose up in Johnny; boredom. It was followed swiftly by its cousin despair as Johnny's search yielded no sign of his precious VR.

As he deftly sifted and scraped through endless mounds of trash, Johnny's mind wandered, conjuring up all the tragedy of the Boneyard. *Lotta history here. Lotta ghost stories too.*

Despite its name, the Heap passed for a city, a place where people worked and lived. If you could call it living. The same couldn't be said of the Boneyard. Birthed of the same mountainous dregs that gave the Heap its unglamorous moniker, it marked the beginning of an era...or perhaps the end of one.

Long before the human race expanded into the broader universe through the Gates, mammoth machines that took advantage of tears in space/time to cheat physics and travel faster than light along slipstream channels, humanity had used up Old Earth. Rather than learning their lesson, they repeated the pattern across the stars, using up world after world. It took almost a century traveling through slipsteam before Recyclers and Chem-Rad sanitation nearly removed the need for waste, human or otherwise.

By the time the Dynasty came to rule the Eight-Fold System, humanity produced a lot of shit.

Johnny let out a tired laugh at the thought then froze, his bark echoing in the stillness. Calming down, Johnny kept sifting.

Humanity found the Eight-Fold System a little over a century and a half before Johnny was even a lustful twinkle in his parents' eyes. A fertile set of stars and planets connected by a little loop of slipstream. When you translated the ludicrously complex mathematics of interstellar travel into simple human concepts, the tangled nest looked like an eight tipped over on its side, one big bunch of pretzeled infinity. A corner pocket galaxy.

Hungry colonists set up shop in a heady rush, eager to grab a piece of dirt to call their own. When the Terran Alliance, the interworlds government that had funded the colonial efforts, came to lay claim to their piece of the cosmos per the deal, the local leaders weren't happy about the bill coming due. The local bosses had enjoyed a few generations of uncontested rule and weren't looking to give it up. What followed was a little dust up called the Glorious War of Liberation and when the smoke cleared the Terrans were forced out by a woman known only as the Empress. Her followers had forged a new government, the Eight-Fold Dynasty, which ruled with justice and honor.

At least according to the Dynastic Nobles who ran the place.

Johnny sneered. *Right. The Dynasty assures all us good little kids in school that they're kind and benevolent overlords. Bullshit. Well, at least they're polite while putting the boots to us. Noblesse oblige and all that.* Johnny felt a buzz in the back of his skull, a dull ache that seemed to ride all the way down his spine. His mind was spinning and spinning and going nowhere, dredging up old stories and ancient history lessons as his hands moved of their own accord. Johnny's mind was running from something and he was okay to let it kept on racing. He's made a lifetime habit of avoiding introspection.

In the aftermath of Terra's defeat and their subsequent banishment from the Eight-Fold System with the Gates destroyed, the Empress and her loyal nobles wanted to clean up the conquered worlds previously held by the Terran Alliance and impress upon their new subjects that their new feudal overlords were preferable to the last ones. But even the wise and infallible Empress couldn't completely fix the former colony of humanity's distant cradle.

Some of the trash could be recycled, slagged, or molecularly condensed, but not all. There was simply too much of it. They couldn't bury it deep enough, couldn't burn it fast enough because the ash and fumes were even worse. So they decided to dump it. Somewhere cheap. Somewhere dingy.

Those criteria meant less-than-fabled Kadath was the chosen dumping ground, an unremarkable mudball made worthwhile only by its relative galactic nearness to most of the other planets that mattered in the Eight-Fold System. Little Kadath wasn't that developed, it wasn't that populated, it didn't even have that picturesque quality some of the more verdant worlds offered. But the planet was conveniently located next door to all its richer neighbors.

Of course, people protested. They protested and they fought back. But no one important, no one with money, no one with power gave a damn. The Empress decreed it done and thus it was so. A whole city got buried, along with the protestors, giving birth to the rancid heart of the Heap.

The Boneyard. A graveyard to the belief that the little people mattered. Even as the junkpile spread out, eating other cities and becoming the megapolis known as the Heap, most folks stayed away from the ruined center. Too many reminders that there used to be humans under the scrap. Too many ghosts. Everyone stayed well clear of the place except the desperate and the crazy.

So that left Johnny, digging through the discarded afterthoughts of an empire reaching for the stars. Half the shit was non-biodegradable metals and plastics. Not plas-steel, or ceramite, or hypertension fibers. Only plain plastic and metal. Untouched by cellular bonding and nanite augmentation. Old, useless, worn out, forgotten, and obsolete.

But one man's trash...

Johnny hissed in pain and shook out his hands after scraping them on some rusted-out sheet of metal.

Great. Getting the shakes. Johnny stared at his jittering hands in morbid fascination. *Thought that happened to other people. To junkies and burnouts.*

He tried to imagine how it had come to this. From respected vid-man and finest shock-jockey in the business to grubbing through trash for a fix.

Face it J.C., you've hit rock bottom. Maybe I'm better off dead.

While Johnny imitated a neo-postmodern Hamlet, an ominous thump and scrape of metal on metal resounded from around the corner of piled debris. A half-life of instincts honed in the slums of the Heap kicked in. Without thinking, the former shock-jock scrambled his bony ass to cover before peeking out from his impromptu haven.

Huh. Like that spy VR bit a few weeks back. Wish I had that tux. Before Johnny's mind became too lost in hazy snippets of stolen memories, something shambled into view.

It was the size of a small mountain. Vaguely man-shaped, but too big and too uneven. It moved with a limp, thumping ungracefully along. Muscles swelled with stimm glands, hypersteroid, and other chemical and cybernetic implants designed to push the human musculature beyond its limits. The thing was as bulky as an Auggie, those artificially augmented heavy laborers and warriors ubiquitous throughout Dynasty worlds, but somehow fundamentally wrong. Like something half put together and then abandoned. The shuffling creature had none of the sleek lethality of the gene-engineered Corps Hunters or the Ruinous Hand, the Empress' trained lunatics. Calling such a thing an Auggie was like calling a jumbled tower of concrete, rebar, and glass a house. This beast was a lump of unfinished muscle, gristle, and fat. Johnny didn't know what it was, but it wasn't an Auggie.

A thick black apron stretched over worker's coveralls, both garments straining to keep its bulk contained. Cruel instruments hung on the coveralls. A wrench sat in one pocket, red tinted surgeon's blade in another. Hammers, saws, and other wicked things. All tools found in hell's kingdom.

Pride of place went to thick loops of chain wrapped around it's wrist, ending in a vicious looking hook. The curved metal instrument was the kind used by meat-tenders, large enough to hang whole carcasses of slaughtered beasts on. Though as befouled as anything else on the shuffling monster, the hook shone, its red stains arranged like marks of pride rather than neglect.

The thing scanned the area, face hidden behind a soiled pig mask. Its rictus caricature of a grinning hog reminded Johnny of Smiler, both grins false and cruel. Rough cord-marked sutures wound haphazardly across the mask, barbed wire stitching holding the rotten material together. A large wet sack hung about the monster's shoulders, flies buzzing all around it.

It looked like a nightmare birthed from the Boneyard itself.

About then, Johnny decided he wanted to live.

As the hulking brute reached his hiding spot, Johnny lunged past the thing. Pig-Face dropped his sack with a wet squelch and reached out with a hand the size of Johnny's head, missing the fleeing junkie by inches.

A terrifying game of cat and mouse ensued amidst the piles and heaps of discarded civilization. A deadly round of tag, with the porcine faced creature definitely "It." The malformed beast-man chased Johnny through twisting caverns of trash, moving with a relentless speed that belied its off-kilter bulk.

Time and again, the huffing monster behind him came almost with reach, the fetid odor of the bloody pursuer washing over Johnny like a dank cloud. The thump-stomp of its thunderous tread and jangling

blades rang in Johnny's ears, almost as loud the fleeing shock-jock's straining heart and lungs.

Even amidst the terror and hammering heartbeat, Johnny felt a rush as good as any VR hit he'd
had.

*Sweet Fates, this is awesome! It's like Stunt Driver
Johnny all over again! Wish someone could record this
chase scene. I'd play that VR all day. Then I'd be me, reliving me. The ultimate Vicarious Reality high.* The thought
of reliving his own VR high made Johnny sloppy,
and he was almost bowled over as the hulking thing
chasing him crashed through a pile of piping with
a sound like a thousand discordant bells. Metal
bits bounced all around Johnny and the Boneyard
stalker got close enough to grab at Johnny's flapping
coat. *Shit, almost got me. Move, Johnny, move!*

The thrill was so good, Johnny didn't want it
to end. He turned tight corners of junk, squeezed
through uneven gaps in leaning towers of junk, and
rolled under jagged limbo bars of broken industrial saws wider than park benches. Johnny's lungs
burned and his muscles ached as he pushed his atrophied and malnourished form harder than he had
in years. Still, Johnny wouldn't stop, couldn't stop,
riding the high for all it was worth.

That high came to a crashing halt when the fleeing junkie slammed into a dead end. Hemmed in on
three sides by the rusted and crumpled skeletons of

cars and aeroships, Johnny looked frantically about. A wet chuckle announced the bone-picker had caught up to his prey.

Only way is up!

Without looking back, Johnny scrambled up the piles of metal. Half way up the rusting mountain, a sharp pain tore through his back and Johnny found himself suddenly and savagely yanked from his perch. A bad joke flashed through the former shock-jock's skull as he tumbled, a remnant from his first and only sky diving adventure; it's not the fall that gets ya...it's the sudden stop at the end.

As a huge shape blocked out the sky, Johnny groggily looked up and saw a length of chain in the monster's hand, ending in a wicked carmine stained hook, glistening with fresh blood.

Sonuvabitchfishhookedme. The last thing Johnny saw was a big filth-encrusted boot coming down to kiss him goodnight.

CHAPTER 2:
A BUTCHER'S LAIR

JOHNNY C. VID woke to an unmerciful scene change, harsher than any of his VR come downs. As his eyes painfully flicker open, a vision of hell greeted him.

A metal cavern, lit by flickering florescent strips and foul-smelling lumps of candles. Rust and oil coated everything, red and black stains on stripped metal. Hooks and chains dangled from the ceiling, with people, corpses, and those in between life and death hung from them like slabs of meat in a larder. There was a sadistic artistry in it, the pained grimaces etched into each bodies' face a grim testament to how each hook dragged the greatest pain from the dangling victims before their end. No gentle peace here, no final rest. Only an ignoble and painful end.

Worse still awaited Johnny's eyes as they drifted from the heavens to the ground.

A hodgepodge of restaurant tables, hydraulic lifts, and surgeon's chairs sat in a circle, each one holding a bound victim. Their restraints were as innovative and varied as their tortures. Barbed wire woven through flesh, arms and legs bound at torturous angles by heavy chain, a few even nailed in place. For all their varieties, the result of the twisted restraints remained constant, offerings on a macabre altar. Some of the trapped victims moved. Some didn't. The buzz of flies and steady drip of unmentionable fluids filled the air. Johnny gagged on the charnel house stench, memories of suffering he'd long buried rushing back with the all too familiar sights and smells. *Please, no. No more. Don't make me remember. I can't. No more death. Oh gods, I need a hit, give me some VR. Please, please, anything to make it all go away.*

Head swiveling, Johnny's eyes stared in blank shock at his surroundings as he froze in horrified fascination. Ancient sensibilities, the vestigial remains of his journalistic skills, awakened in Johnny's stunned brain, analyzing and categorizing what the trapped junkie numbly witnessed. The beast's lair, for it was certainly that, was a labor of love in its own twisted way. The disparate pieces gathered together demonstrated patient and meticulous effort.

Crude wield marks showed a personal touch on the restraints and torture devices. Mattresses and construction sheeting covered the walls as a kind of primitive and brutish sound muffling.

So no one can hear the screams. Johnny tried to leap off the table only to be violently halted by leather straps. Trapped by the thick bands, the shock-jock wiggled his head about, desperately searching for a way out from this house of horrors. Only sorrow and death greeted Johnny.

Their host entered with a creak of rusted hinges and a clanging thunk of heavy locks. Without even looking at its victims, the monster stomped over to a work desk, back turned to the captive audience. With a tug and a grunt, the misshapen creature removed its mask, placing the porcine false-face aside as it worked on some foul project. Craning against the straps, Johnny could barely see his kidnapper out the corner of his eye.

The mask had nothing on the monster's ugly mug. Molted and warped like clay, muscles twitched and veins bulged. Scars crisscrossed mottled flesh, mirroring the barbed wire of its false face. Tumorous growths completely covered one eye while the other glared about, a dark pit of malice. A killer's face, a beast's face. Brutal and ugly as the pit it dwelt in. And it was looking right at Johnny.

Johnny flinched and choked down panic as the bloody thing shuffled toward him. His mind raced desperately, trying to process a way out. Nothing in his life prepared him to face such a monster. All Johnny had to draw on was the shattered remnants of VR, fading bits of other people people's memories. The junkie dug through the stolen memories that remained with desperate speed, finding refuge in stolen victories. *Okay, okay, okay. I got this. I'll just...just... pretend this is a Boom-Boom flick. Action scene. Yeah, this is where our hero gets the drop on him! Commando Johnny.*

A balled fist upside the head interrupted ol' Johnny's inner monologue. Pig-Face slung the dazed man across his shoulder in a fireman's carry. A musk of oil, blood, and chemical sweat hung oppressively about the beast. With a casual and deliberate slowness, the monster picked through hanging chains, their rattling like the windchimes of the damned, until it settled on an empty hook, stained red with years of gruesome use. The bloated creature cradled it with a reverent tenderness, running a calloused thumb along its curves, testing its point. Johnny fought down a wave of nausea and told himself he was just biding his time, ready to strike. When the rusty hook tore through his shoulder, a startling and terrifying realization rushed over Johnny riding a wave of pain.

With it came a rush of unkind enlightenment, a painful revelation for the writhing shock-jock. The beast could have gutted Johnny or anyone of the other victims. It could have used any the sharp things, things made for ending, that it carried around.

But it didn't. It wanted them to live. To suffer. It wanted their pain to last.

This wasn't an action flick. It was a horror movie, with Johnny cast as the helpless victim.

"Nononono, please, please, please don't do this. You can't. I'll do anything, please don't make me an extra in my own life!" Numb fingers clawed at the chain as the former shock-jock gibbered.

His pleading earned him a sadistic snicker and a push from Pig-Face, sending Johnny swinging. Johnny choked, a panicked gurgle, gulping for air through the pain as the sharp hook dug deeper. Johnny could feel the wicked point, pushing aside meat and bone, sending waves of nausea and agony through Johnny's body. His eyes blurred and vomit rise in his gorge as he swayed next to the decaying remains of a previous victim. Flies buzzed in open sockets, the soft bits rancid and devoured by the carrion eaters.

Fates no, I can't end like this. Not a hero. Not even a bystander. Just one more faceless victim, a tally on some sick bastard's body count.

Thrashing from one of the other tables diverted Johnny's tormentor away from its current game.

Pig-Face turned from Johnny, a merciful moment of respite. One of the victims struggled as Pig-Face's cruel devices did their work. Death spasms. The last moments before the lights go out.

Seen too many of those not to recognize it. Bitter memories, all too real and belonging only to Johnny, washed over the trapped Mr. Vid. All the suffering he hid from, buried in his many VR trips through other people's lives. All the blood. All the bodies. Tiny little hands, reaching out, begging, pleading for help as life faded from their eyes.

Pig-Face, looming over the thrashing corpse-to-be, uttered a low chortle, a nasty, satisfied sound. Hanging like a piece of meat, Johnny shivered. *Looks like I'm not the only one who knows the Reaper's Shadow when they see it.* The beast's hunger was real; it slavered like a junkyard dog with a steak. Johnny squinted suspiciously. There was something familiar about that as well.

The bone picker dug about its own skullcase, fishing through the flabs of fat and meat to pull out a brutal-looking spike. With a snort, the beast plunged it into the victim's port. Burrowed into the dying soul's brain, Pig-Face's eyes rolled back with a heavy huff of ecstasy, nostrils flaring and mouth hanging open like a dog.

Hung on his chain, Johnny's eyes widened. *I know that look, too. A junkie getting his fix. The bastard is getting off by living through their pain.*

As the final moments passed and Pig-Face callously dumped the body down a metal chute with no more thought than throwing out the trash, it hit Johnny where the Smiler got his product.

Dead Play. Ghoul Records. Scavenging the cure bastard's leftovers.

Trapped in a madman's playground, Johnny clutched at that realization. It fed his anger, burning away his despair. *I can't die here. I have to kill this bastard. I have to live long enough to punch Smiler in his ugly face.* Bitterness and hate helped Johnny fight through the agony as he hauled himself around on the hook. He nearly passed out from the pain. Scratching around his brain case, the shock-jock scrambled to find his port. Thankfully the skin was thin, the implant puffy, raw, its mechanisms easy to reach. Another sign of how far Johnny had gone down the rabbithole.

Damn, never thought I'd be grateful to be a junkie. He flicked a few physical bits around before mentally running through his cyberware's settings; tiny checkboxes clicking off and on behind Johnny's eyes. Digital switches going to and fro. Set system to record. Something he swore off since...

Since I started running from life.

His desperate gamble kicked into motion, Johnny had to bait the trap. He thrashed and choked, wiggling like a fish on a hook. The monster shuffled back, a shark drawn to blood. Johnny could practically hear its thoughts. *'Another? So soon? I really shouldn't...but why turn down a gift?'*

C'mon you gluttonous bastard. Only us junkies here. Come get your fix. Ungentle hands steadied the dangling captive and Pig-Face plunged its metal spike into Johnny's port, ready to taste the darkness and despair of a living creature's final moments, the sweet suffering of the fading soul. Instead, the creature found itself sucking down static. Caught in a feedback loop, back and forth, like a hall of mirrors in its brain.

His brain.

For a moment, Johnny felt the monster's mind, riding on the feedback pain of rusty nails scratching through his brain. Hunger, rage, agony, and blood-lust.

Pig-Face howled, squealing like his mask's namesake, and threw Johnny to the side. The murderer thrashed blindly about his abattoir lair as Johnny struggled to breathe. Pain near paralyzed the would-be victim.

Sweet merciful stars, never been on the other end of it. Can't stop. Can't pass out. Gotta move. A small eternity passed as Vid inched along the floor with one good arm, leaving a trail of crimson behind him. Johnny reached a dirty patch of rubber beneath the chute. As his trembling fingers gripped the soiled lip of his escape, a bellow of rage and the whining roar of a friction-blade buzzing to life erupted behind him. Johnny turned his head, a tiny movement, but enough to send black spots dancing in his eyes. It didn't prevent him from seeing the blood chilling sight behind him.

The monster's one eye, bloodshot and burning with hate, fixed on the struggling escapee. A huge whirring blade, designed to carve through sheet metal, waved about with evil intent.

With a desperate surge of adrenaline, Johnny flung himself into the chute, tumbling end over end, as the pneumatic delivery system shunted him through what felt like miles of pitch-black tubing. As new light erupted about him, Johnny found himself falling toward a mountain of corpses. Glassy eyes filled his vision before darkness took him.

Consciousness came and went and with it waves of nausea and pain. Johnny struggled to hang on, to focus on something to keep himself from slipping back into oblivion.

Smiler whistled jauntily to himself as he walked through this little macabre corner of the Boneyard. The sleazy corpsepicker even talked to himself, singsong and chipper. Johnny heard him call the corpse pile "his secret garden."

"No one comes here, no need to care. We don't have to worry none, not until we are done." The familiar voice, the gloating of the smug piece of shit who sent Johnny straight into the Butcher's arms gave the dying shock-jock the focus he needed, a burst of pure rage and hatred that hit the dying embers of his life like napalm. Still singing, Smiler trotted closer to Johnny's nearly final resting place. "Butcher takes the meat, juicy sweet. When it's done, we get some. Oh yes, dear chum!"

Picking through mounds of broken bodies and bits of metal in his purple suit, Smiler practically lit up when he happened across a familiar face slouched on top of the mound. His most regular patron, Johnny C. Vid. Who, unbeknownst to the garishly dressed pusher, watched through closed eyes. Smiler chuckled to himself. "This day keeps getting better and better."

Johnny kept perfectly still as the little goblin hopped over to his spot at the top of the corpse mound, picking his way daintily over the juicier bits. The pusher knelt down with a small chuckle. "Sorry, Johnny boy. Guess your little entrepreneurial venture didn't come too much, eh chum?" Smiler paused as though he'd expected an answer. "Pity, really. Your creds were good but I know when a junkie is at his limit. I can always pick 'em. I mean, c'mon buddy. Desperate enough to hit the Boneyard for a fix?" Another chortle at the former shock-jock's expense and Smiler reached down to start looting Johnny's body. "You really were in a bad way."

To say Smiler was surprised when Johnny reached out to grab him by the throat with feverish strength would be an understatement. To say Smiler shit himself in surprise when the undead Johnny rose, blackened and bedraggled, to glare at Smiler with bloodshot eyes would not be an exaggeration.

"I've seen better days." Johnny rasped out. He could barely keep his eyes open but focused everything he had to keep his hands locked around the pusher's throat.

"But I think you're going to have an even worse one, you little carrion-eating piece of shit. Looks like you and your piggy masked buddy's plan didn't work." A wracking cough shook the half-dead shock-jock to the core. "I'm gonna do you like he does your victims."

Smiler feebly tried to protest his innocence. "You got it all wrong! Look, I just get the left overs. Ol' Piggly Wiggly does his thing and Smiler just picks up the pieces. I'm just looking out for number one. You know how it is, man. That's the way it goes in the Heap." The purple suited pusher scratched frantically at the vice around his neck. Grimy nails left bloody furrows on Johnny C. Vid's arm but Smiler couldn't dislodge his former client's death grip. With his desperate appeal to mercy foiled, Smiler turned to desperate pleading.

"Hey, hey, Smiler's always been there for you, buddy! Let me go and I'll give ya a free hit!"

Johnny sneered at Smiler's begging. *This must be what I looked like.* With a final squeeze, Johnny let the little worm go. Not because he wanted to but because the wrecked shock-jock couldn't muster up the strength to wring the bastard's neck. Smiler scurried off as Johnny pulled himself off the mound.

Slowly.

As he crawled down the pile of the dead, Johnny laughed, a harsh bark that echoed eerily in the city-sized graveyard. He'd never felt so alive. Being so close to death and madness had jump-started his system. When Smiler offered Johnny the hit, he hadn't even wanted it.

I'll be sure to come back and thank you, my pig-faced friend.

Johnny intended to show his gratitude appropriately...by hunting the misshapen bastard down and killing him. Thoughts of revenge kept the chill evening at bay as Johnny C. Vid, Heap dweller and former VR junkie, shuffled into the night to heal and plot his revenge.

CHAPTER 3:
A New Lease on Life

EVEN IN THE HEAP it wasn't common to see someone half dead stumble into a street clinic. Even stranger to see that person laughing their head off at the same time. Usually the ones doing the laughing had buried the body in a hole somewhere and never needed immediate and urgent medical attention.

The street clinic staff paused uncertainly, not sure if they should be whisking the laughing man off to the psych ward or the ER. That lasted until the newcomer collapsed onto the worn tile after shoving a handful of coins and cred cards at a nearby orderly.

That got the staff moving in a hurry.

Johnny was raced to the ER and subjected to the tender affections of the tired and overworked staff.

The shock-jock remembered little but he did recall a chain-smoking doctor cursing at him regularly as she plugged up the bleeding holes in his body. A steady feed of enhanced plasma refilled the precious red fluid Johnny had left in a crimson trail from the monster's lair. Antibiotics took care of any lingering viruses and bacteria. The doctors even cloned new meat and bone to replace the hole in Johnny's shoulder. Sewed him up, good as new. All paid for courtesy of the coins and credits left by Smiler in his hasty retreat.

I'll have to thank the little shit when I find him again by ripping out his lungs.

Patched up and no longer at risk of immediately expiring, Johnny was then subjected to the hard stuff.

Rehabilitation.

Johnny winced as he raised a small squishy ball, squeezed hard, and put it back down again. Like he had a thousand times before and would a thousand times more. Next to his bedside a bored orderly kept up a steady drone of monotone encouragement. "Good. That's it. Keep going. You can do this. Now, again."

Johnny shook his head and wiped beads of sweat from his forehead with his good arm. If he dropped the ball even a little the orderly gave him hell for it. *Sweet Fates, if this keeps up I really will go insane.*

Johnny had been fortunate since his recovery. When he first stumbled in, Johnny'd been spilling his guts about the carnival of nightmares he's faced in the Boneyard, including its chem-enhanced ringmaster. His ramblings of a pig-faced maniac were written off as trauma and the side effects of the potent mix of painkillers they'd pumped into Mr. Vid. When he'd come to his senses and the delicate questions came, Johnny played dumb.

That's the only reason I'm not under psychiatric watch.

Convinced Johnny wasn't stark raving bonkers and deemed as whatever passed for sane in the Heap, the kind clinic orderlies only watched him like a hawk to make sure his recovery proceeded apace. Though if the brutalized shock-jock did stick around a bit too long, they'd be happy to add a few extra zeros to his tab. Johnny felt an especial burden to recover, particularly once he considered the costs he was racking up. The golden trinkets that tumbled from Smiler had been all used up saving Johnny's miserable life and the bedridden shock-jock didn't have any line of Dynasty creds to lean on.

So, unsurprisingly, as Mr. Vid's health improved, his mood deteriorated.

Johnny C. Vid, the man, the myth, the legend knew he couldn't wait for the long rehabilitative recovery, couldn't even hope to afford it, and couldn't take the Butcher on even if he avoided debtor's organ harvesting.

Butcher. The name Johnny gave the thing. It was the only thing that fit. *Pig-Face doesn't do that monster justice.* He'd thought about it a lot during his rehabilitation. Wasn't much to do but think.

Even if I wasn't slagged out and only skin and bone, I'm gonna need more than a few pushups and a power drink to take the Butcher on. I need an edge if I want that freak dead.

And Johnny very much wanted the killer dead. Johnny pondered his situation, day by day, hour by hour, thoughts moving to the ticking of the clock. Weeks went by, racking up credit and wracking Johnny's brain as he tumbled the thoughts in his head over and over and over again.

The Butcher had tried to kill him and Johnny couldn't simply count his blessings and move on with his life. No, it wasn't just that the Butcher tried to kill Johnny, it was that in doing so the thing proved it had only been trying to kill a husk. The pig-faced bastardhad brought into terrible clarity that Johnny stopped living a long time ago. The good Mr. Vid had simply continued to breathe.

Dammit, I started the VR so I could keep on living without putting a bullet through my skull. When did my life take a backseat to the virtual?

Johnny's best guess was when the nightmares started.

While at the peak of his shock-jock career with Public Eye Media, Johnny had slowly burned himself out, falling deeper into a spiral of depression even as he climbed the heights of fame and wealth. The profits Johnny made on robbing the dead of their dignity in lurid vid-casts tore at him. The dead haunted him in his dreams, eyes accusing, hands grasping. Johnny told himself it didn't matter, that there was nothing he could do to change things. He wasn't responsible for their woes. The shock-jock might as well help himself, making something good out of their misfortune. Still, it got harder for Johnny to do his job. To get the best shot on yet more glass-eyed children to satisfy the numb and hungry masses, to grin an empty grin as he interviewed a weeping mother, and crack another gallows humor joke as lives were ruined.

So J.C. Vid started in on the VR, using stolen memories just to feel something untouched by guilt and pain. Then it became the only thing Johnny could feel. He'd lost his job, his friends, and his home. But it hadn't mattered, because he was living someone else's life even as he lost his own.

The Butcher stole even that sweet lie from him. Punctuated his little bubble of oblivion and forced Johnny to confront the wreck his life had become and the ghosts of his previous celebrity. The absence of it all, fame, fortune, and even dignity, weighed him down as surely as an anchor tied round his neck.

The memory of glassy eyes in the Boneyard's mound of dead haunted Johnny as he sat in his hospital bed, hopped up on painkillers and waiting for his body to grow strong again. The dead glared at him as accusingly as the ones in his old nightmares. Lucky bastard, they sang, you're a dead man walking and you still get to keep breathing. Why couldn't we be so lucky? You don't deserve your life and we didn't deserve to die!

Johnny couldn't bring back the dead back but he could stop the murderous creature that left a trail of death in its wake. Not that it was a selfless act on Johnny's part. Altruism didn't sit too well with Mr. Vid. But obsession, addiction, and revenge did. The potent cocktail drove away every other hunger, even his need for VR.

I'm alive, dammit. I'm gonna prove I'm alive and that this life is mine to live. I'm gonna get those ghosts to finally quiet down. And I'm going to do it by killing the Butcher.

Johnny fumed, plotted, and obsessed over the Butcher. Revenge consumed him.

In the end, there was really only one option. One terribly risky option. The former shock-jock stared at the stained ceiling and its sterile fluorescent lights. *Am I willing to sell my soul for revenge?*

Yes.

Johnny struggled up his hospital bed to painstakingly grab his comm-pad lying on the rickety end table. A few pounds of the digits and Johnny reached out to get in touch an old fan, by way of one blackmailed old mafia stool pigeon.

"Hey Paul-Chen, its Johnny. Long time no speak. Hope protective custody's working out for you. Which brings me to why I called. Yep, I'm cashing in that favor. Now, now don't make a fuss. That was my price for getting you out of the Bangkok Quarter without selling you off to the highest bidder. It was my skin on the line just as much as yours. No backing out now. We had an agreement. I can call up any of the old warlords in a heartbeat. You remember, Williams, don't you? The one that liked to collect fingers?" Johnny waited for the blubbering to die down on the other end of the line. "You finished? Good. I need you to dig out some digits for your old Triad buddies. I want to get in touch with Elder Dang."

≈

A few clandestine calls using the contact info purloined from shaking down Paul-Chen and Johnny C. Vid was on the fast track to talking with the Triads.

It didn't take long for them to send someone out to talk. The crime families were always eager to help a new client make questionable life choices.

The Triad representative who arrived did not look like Johnny expected. Oh sure, he had the ubiquitous black suit that foot soldiers of the Triads favored, regardless of which of the rival families they came from, but everything from there diverged sharply from expectations.

It was clear this was not your average Triad.

The rep had shown up in Johnny's room with a knock on the door and an easy grin. The Triad's head was covered in a peach fuzz, a lazy monk's headspace, the hair of a man a stone's throw from enlightenment. Square glasses with multicolored lens that cycled through a rainbow of colors, stylish and immensely flashy, almost covered up the man's laugh lines rested on a sun-tanned face above an easy smile. A shirt reading "I'd rather be fishing!" covered a comfortable gut and any lingering mirage of professionalism granted by the crisp business jacket finally died completely where the sable cloth hit orange board shorts patterned with a wavy sunset.

Pretty damn far from the sterling image of a ruthless Triad agent.

What the hell kind of ruthless, soulless, professional representative of a criminal organization wears flip-flops?

The Triad representative slouched into the room and pulled up a chair, leaning back with a pleased sigh. "J.C. Vid, I presume? Name's S-Pos, Triad representative in the area. You can call me 'Da Pos.'" When

Johnny made no attempt to do so, the fuzzy headed Triad looked the bed ridden shock-jock up and
down. "You look like hell, brudda."

Johnny grunted and raised himself up as best he
could. "I've had better days."

"Hope so or that's some shitty way to live." S-Pos
pulled out a sleek data-slate that looked ten times
as valuable as the man working it. "Gotta say, I'm
impressed. You got some good contacts for someone
outside of the family." S-Pos looked over the slate,
eyes suddenly sharp behind his glasses, reminding
Johnny the first lesson he'd learned in the journalist
and entertainment industry; looks could be deceiv-
ing. *How many people has this S-Pos guy shoved a knife
into while grinning like their best friend?* "How does a
guy like you know the number of Elder Dang's personal secretary?"

"Elder Hoa Dang was a rabid follower of my career when I was a shock-jock with the Public Eye.
He used to send letters my way, saying how he appreciated my work, big fan, yadda yadda. Told me
to keep in touch." Johnny adopted an air of causal
disinterest frowned inwardly. *It creeped me the hell out,
having a mafia don send fan mail. Not that this guy needs
to know that.*

"Hmm. Yeah, Elder Dang did always talk you up.
Best shock-jock in the biz according to the boss."
The board short clad Triad scratched his stubble and

consulted his slate. Johnny did his best not to sweat bullets as S-Pos took his sweet time. "Which brings me to my next question. Ya know, the five million credit one. Why are you reaching out to Elder Dang now? It's been a while since you had prime billing on the Net, ya know?"

Johnny decided to let the observation of the painfully obvious slide. Especially since he was the one coming to the Triads with hat in hand to beg a favor. "I need some serious rejuvenat treatment."

"Damn, son. I knew the show biz industry was harsh but it's a bit much to contact the Triads to get yourself pretty again, ya know?"

At that little flippant remark, Johnny let some heat show. "This isn't about my damn career. I need what the Triads have to make me stronger, faster, and tougher than I've ever been. I need the heaviest hardware you can get and then some."

Johnny's little outburst grabbed S-Pos's attention. The shaved headed Triad sat forward, elbows on knees, eager for more. "That's gonna take some serious scratch. Who do you want dead?"

No beating around the bush. "The same guy who did this to me."

"That must be some nasty sunavabitch to need the kinda juice you're asking for."

"You don't know the half of it."

After taking a moment to ensure the two had the privacy you'd expect when a Triad walks into a room in the Heap, Johnny gave S-Pos the lowdown on the Butcher; from running into the shambling thing in the Boneyard to Johnny's harrowing scrape with death. It felt good to tell someone else, to vent the bile and rage. It never come close to exorcising it, but it made it real. A promise, somehow, to give voice to it, to tell someone else.

Da Pos sat and nodded and didn't say a word. He didn't have to. The Triad agent's face said it all. *He can think I'm nuts or high on drugs all he wants. I just need him to get me to Elder Dang.*

Regardless of his opinion of Johnny's mental state, the Triad representative listened, nodded, and frequently consulted his sleek data-slate, making notes and tallying up the total bill. S-Pos may have thought Johnny was crazy but the Triads didn't let a little thing like insanity that get in the way of business. *Guess he really is a professional. Even if he wears board shorts.*

"You know this won't come cheap and it won't come easy. You ain't got two credits to rub together. The Triads are going to own you."

"This isn't my first rodeo, Mr. Pos. I know what I'm signing up for. I still want in. The pig-faced fuck has to die."

Da Pos grinned. He grinned in a way that fisherman do when they've snagged a large catch. *Yeah, a big wiggling junkie shock-jock. Long as he doesn't string me up like the Butcher and gets me what I need, I couldn't care less. I chose this.*

"Sounds good to me, brudda. Put your thumb here, here, and here...thank you. There. All done."

Johnny blinked. "That's it? Don't you guys need a blood oath or teach me the secret handshake for an initiation ceremony or something?"

S-Pos laughed and patted the slate affectionately. "Nah, we got it all streamlined now. Bargain is sealed and recognized. I've sent out a notice to some good doctors who work for us. They'll get you patched up better than new." The sharpness returned as S-Pos hit Johnny with his sharkish grin. "You'll get yours my friend, and then the Triads get you."

Johnny's release went swimmingly after that. The Triads whisked him away from the free clinic, settling any lingering debts with brusque efficiency. Coins switched hands, hard currency utilized in lieu of Dynasty credits. Though hard wealth was frowned upon for official Dynastic business, it was still a semi-official currency, a necessity in a star spanning empire. Distance and sheer diversity among the scattered worlds, governments, and peoples of the Eight-Fold System meant having something more tangible on hand as a backup. Sometimes the good officials just couldn't be there all the time. The Dynasty minted a selection of its own coins to use in official transfers but a plethora of other shining gewgaws served just as well, from gold ingots and shimmering gems to pre-Dynasty coinage.

In the Heap and other places where folks and things slipped through the cracks in the Dynasty's shining bureaucracy, these baubles were the currency of choice.

The official cred-of-the-realm was all fine and good but other, more liquid and less traceable assets, were the Triads preferred payment. The underpaid and overworked staff were imminently familiar with backdoor deals to make a patient disappear. It seemed the Hippocratic oath didn't stand up so well to the combination of a loaded gun and a fat purse.

Johnny mused on the doctor's dilemma as he sat in the back of a black four-wheeled monstrosity, surrounded by black and red suited Triad goons. *Not like they could stop the Triad goons anyway. And the nobles who fund these things don't care as long as the façade of their good deeds remains intact.*

Johnny pondered all this as he stared at his haggard reflection in the mirrorshades of the scowling slab of muscle sitting to his left until a curt grunt from the Triad foot solider encourage the shock-jock to turn his eyes elsewhere.

Free clinics are funny that way. A place where the best and worst of intentions shake hands and mingle. The Dynast nobles fund places to care for the people they get rich off of, showing how much they care for us poor little peasants. Of course, this noblesse oblige doesn't go nearly far enough, so you have black markets to fill in the gaps. Enter, the Triads.

Johnny snuck another glance at the very scary men and women currently guarding their honored guest. *These bastards are no better than the Dynasts. Oh sure, the Triad families will do you a solid. Get you whatever you need. But it'll cost you.* Johnny snorted to himself, earning another grunt, this time from the guard on his right. *No appreciation for my refined observations... even if they're all in my head. They probably think I should be grateful. Without them, I wouldn't stand a chance at getting back at that pig-faced bastard. Yeah. Grateful. I'd be so much more grateful if they skipped that whole blood oath and the promised bullet to the brain if I screw up.*

"Hey, brudda, snap out of it. No more daydreaming. We're here."

Johnny's head snapped up at S-Pos lazy drawl. The Triad vehicle had stopped in front of an unassuming office building. Squat, ugly, and utterly desolate. Whatever color it used to possess had faded to a dingy yellowing gray-green, smog and the elements leaving their mark on the unremarkable cube.

"We're stopping here?"

S-Pos grin could have melted butter. "Yep. You like it?"

"It's uglier than the skinmap of a diehard pain-freak."

Somehow, the Triad's toothy smile only got wid-er. "Better get used to it, my man. Because until we say so, this little corner of paradise is your new digs."

Johnny glared up at the derelict slice of the Heap, sullen anger and desperation churning in-side of him, choking off the fear rising like bile. Fear of the Butcher. Fear of failing to find the creature. Fear of his nightmares never ending. Finally, John-ny stopped, closed his eyes, and took a deep breath. Chemical exhaust, stale alcohol, piss, and other less identifiable scents hit Johnny's nose. The smells of the Heap, of the streets. Home.

Other smells hit him. The coppery tang of blood. Cold and brittle iron and steel. Chemically tainted sweat. Fear rode those scents and rolled over John-ny like a tidal wave. Some from the Butcher. Some from older pains. Johnny dug deeper, past the fear and into his hate. He opened his eyes and looked at the Triad safehouse with new eyes. *This isn't a place to rest. This is a base, a fortress. I'll heal up. Get stronger. Then, when I'm done, I'm gonna hunt down that pig-faced Butcher and kill him.*

Johnny grimaced as the Butcher's victims swam in his mind, mixed with the cavalcade of horrors from his long and storied career as a shock-jock. *I'll kill him and then maybe I can sleep. No more dead eyes staring at me.*

Johnny looked at S-Pos, who calmly leaned against the sleek black Triad vehicle they rode in, unperturbed and unimpressed with Johnny's silent vows.

The shock-jock sickly grin stared back at him from the multicolored shades of his patron, the face of a deranged Don Quixote on his final quest with Death riding shotgun.

"Home, sweet home."

Chapter 4:
An Unquiet Mind

WEEKS OF REHABILITATION PASSED in a blur of therapy and treatment. The stopgap biowork of the free clinic was refined, built on, and expanded. Phage-nanites and body-scrubbers cleansed the shock-jock's body of a lifetime of poor treatment, getting his circulatory system to peak efficiency. The pump primed, he was then fed a healthy diet of genetically modified nutrient paste, stimms, and other growth chemicals, essentially a reduced version of the program that created an Auggie. Johnny was just grateful they skipped the more invasive surgery, like bleeding out his bones to replace them with steel-marrow injections or scooping out his insides to replace them with newer, better, bulkier bio-mechanical parts. When the chop-docs were done fine tuning his body, Johnny felt like a new man. After that, he experienced the best bedside manner blood money could buy.

Johnny's quarters were small and ugly as the outside, buried in the reinforced guts of the office building. They were, however, well furnished. Roughly as large as a small apartment, Johnny's new home had a personal computer, small weights stashed into a corner for rehab work, a shower stall and even a kitchenette, complete with stove and cold storage. To the former junkie, who hadn't counted on hot running water for the last thirteen months, it was a palace.

The pièce de résistance lay in the bedroom. Claiming nearly all of the ten by ten square was a plush padded rest-slab, a cross between a couch and an advanced surveillance system. The bed was more advanced than anything the free clinic could have hoped to possess. The padding moved, molded, slid, and flexed to support the shock-jock's recovering body, reading his metrics and vitals through a host of sensors monitored whenever Johnny laid down on the thing. The bulky recliner might have been luxurious but it was a necessity to ensure Johnny survived the recovery process. The Triads were exceedingly diligent about monitoring Johnny's vitals. The care and attention rather touched the shock-jock. *They really don't want to lose their investment.*

When Johnny wasn't recovering, he was training.

The Triad sadists masquerading as doctors pushed Johnny to his limits, time and time again. When he protested, they laughed and pushed harder. His new body needed to be worked as it healed, they told him. *I think they just like to see me suffer.*

No facet of physical exercise escaped their tender attentions. Resistance training, body weight, cardio. Stamina work, sprinting, heavy weights, light weights, push, pull, and more besides. It never seemed to end. *I'm pretty sure these bastards are inventing new tortures just to screw with me. Seriously, how many ways can you lift something heavy and put it back down?*

Even if Johnny complained about the Triad doctors' workout regimen, he couldn't complain about the results. Johnny grew stronger, faster, tougher with every painful training session put behind him. Each new benchmark was surpassed to be replaced by a harder challenge only to see it too surpassed. The shock-jock snarled in pained glee every time and dug deeper, fueled by his pain and hatred. *I'm coming for you, Butcher. I'm coming for you and I'm going to end your sorry ass.*

Unsurprisingly, Johnny's mental state wasn't repairing apace with his physique. Though Johnny was healing physically, his mind still bled. The same seething morass of pain, hatred, rage, and fear that kept the vengeful shock-jock running, jumping, and pumping iron day after day after day in the dark concrete bunker festered inside of Johnny like a cancer.

That was part of why Johnny threw himself into the workouts with such fervor. His hatred might have had him sprinting towards his goals, but Johnny was running from his fears just as fast. As much as Johnny dreaded the painful testing, he dreaded the solitude of his room far more. Left in the silence of the evening with only himself, Johnny's thoughts gnawed on themselves like starving rats trapped in a cage.

With night came the dreams.

Johnny never remembered the full details. What he did remember was the haunting cries, choked sobs, and fading screams. The smell of burning flesh, spilled blood, and salted ash. All the remains of what used to be humans. Johnny tasted burnt hopes and destroyed lives dancing on the tip of his tongue, ash, copper, dirt, and dust floating in the air. Weeping and moans echoed in half-ruined cities in a ululating symphony of pain. The dead and dying lay piled together, torn by bullets, gutted by blades, and subjected a thousand fates too cruel to imagine, all screaming their pain to an uncaring world.

Worst of all were the eyes.

They followed Johnny relentlessly. Begging, pleading, blaming. Why, they asked. Why did they suffer while he didn't? How could he walk amongst such horrors and be unscathed? Why, when Johnny had gained fame and fortune, reporting woes with a sick grin on his face for masses, laughing like a ghoulish prophet?

Johnny shook his head, mutely denying them, until the shock-jock couldn't bear their weight any longer. Faced with his guilt, Johnny fled into the desolate hell-city, desperately trying to escape their haunting eyes and begging, outstretched hands.

It never worked.

No matter how fast Johnny ran, no matter where he turned, they were there. Mauled and scarred, breathing or still, they lined the streets like horrible marionettes, jerking and twitching. Johnny knew their face. He knew every one of them. There, the half-charred remains of the thirteenth victim of the Cannibal Baker of Yves stood next to the flensed meat of Jennie Pho, who Johnny interviewed about her abduction by Bonestealer Jacque, forcing her to relive the trauma even as she shivered under a blanket on the bumper of an ambulance.

Sickeningly, these were not new dreams. Old wounds, still festering, buried under a layer of VR for years. What was new was the thunder. A teeth rattling thump-drag that boomed from behind the shock-jock. A foul, warm wind washed over Johnny in his dreams, carrying the scent of rust, blood, and chemicals. The Butcher followed Johnny as he ran, always dogging his steps, chortling obscenely as Johnny screamed for help, before hooks, dozens of rusty hooks, sprang from the shadows to rip and tear at the shock-jock. The end came as it always did, at the hand of Butcher's sadistic tools as the damning eyes of their silent audience watched on.

Strange wonder, then, that Johnny C. Vid, the man, the myth, the legend, dreaded sleep so thoroughly and clung to the pain of his training like a drowning man at driftwood.

One day, as the physical therapists put Johnny through his paces running marathons the old him couldn't have hoped to have tolerated, S-Pos wandered in to pay a visit to his client.

"How you doing, brudda?"

"Doing...great..." Johnny panted each word around an oxygen mask as his feet pounded the treadmill. *My favorite hamster wheel. Going nowhere fast.*

"Good. Docs say you check out alright. Say give you some more time with that new bod of yours. Let your grow into your sea legs. Me, I say fuck that." S-Pos shrugged and waved at the sour faced medical staff. "So, c'mon. Time for the fun stuff."

At a nod from S-Pos, the Triad cyber-docs and chem-heads who monitored Johnny yanked off the host of monitoring equipment and set him loose.

With a grin, the bald-headed Triad crooked a finger and walked down the hall.

Johnny walked behind, moving with the jerky gait of a teenager and feeling the pull of new muscles. Even the skin around his polished up dataport was pink and itchy. *Even with all this physical conditioning, it still feels like I'm wearing a rental two sizes too big or too small.* The docs had told Johnny he'd get used to the beefed-up body. They didn't seem to have a solid time frame for it, though. Soon, eventually, and some day were the closest things to a solid date they could give him. *Can't wait for that to happen. Getting real sick of feeling like I'm going through puberty again, even if I can't argue with the results so far.* Johnny looked down and clenched a fist, muscles taut, savoring the power there. More than Johnny had ever dreamed of while dwelling the fetid streets of the Heap. Then, *that pig-faced freak is mine.*

Once again, S-Pos either didn't notice or didn't care about his walking partner's silent oaths of vengeance and marched along with a grin, flip-flops making echoing slaps in the chilly hallway. He cocked his head back to look at Johnny and his frowning face.

"So, this Chopper guy..."

"Butcher."

Johnny corrected the irreverent Triad, the shock-jock's boiling rage burned into the name he'd bequeathed on the pig-faced murderer.

Not that S-Pos gave any weight to Johnny's trauma soaked hissings, waving a hand like he was shooing away a fly as the two trod down the endless tunnels of the drab safehouse.

"Sure, yeah. This Butcher sounds like a real nasty piece of work. Even if he's only up here." S-Pos never lost his manic grin as tapped his shaven head with two fingers like a melon at a market. "Maybe you're crazy. I mean, you're crazy, brudda, or else you wouldn't have come to us. But maybe that big bad bastard really is out there, y'know? So, we gotta make sure you are prepared."

They came to what looked like a vault door, two Triad guards standing watch like stone dogs at a temple. Johnny hadn't paid them, or the door, much mind in the past. The black suited grunts were ubiquitous in the Heap building. Johnny passed them by without so much as a wave. They had a system; Johnny didn't bother the goons, the goons didn't bother Johnny.

Never went looking into doors I shouldn't. Didn't have the time. The body-docs have a pretty strict regime. Johnny rolled his shoulders. *Not like I care about the Triads dirty secrets now. That might have had the old career-driven J.C. Vid drooling but not anymore.* Johnny shook his head ruefully. *That was a lifetime ago. A different man, a different time. Truth be told, I don't need to know the Triads secrets. I know what I signed up with. A deal with the devil to kill a monster.*

S-Pos exchanged a curt nod with both the guards and strode to the armored door. Like a born showman, S-Pos opened the reinforced steel slab with a huff of effort and waved Johnny inside with a flourish. Johnny's breath caught at the treasure trove inside. Weaponry of all kinds, from blunt objects to advanced firearms lay in rows by the door. Some were hung on racks, others laid out on tables. Still others, mainly crude stabbing and beating weapons were shoved into barrels. The guns ranged from old slug throwers to the weapons that wouldn't look out of place in the hands of the Empress' personal guard.

By the Pure Lands, I haven't seen this much firepower since the Warlord Uprising in the Bangkok Quarter. At least these aren't aimed at me this time. Johnny shot a worried glance at S-Pos, trying to read the crazy Triad's intent. *Not yet, anyway.*

The hardware wasn't there only for show. Well-used training dummies and targets sat on firing ranges made of concrete and bright orange gel-casing, the cheap kind used for crash padding on freeways and racetracks throughout the Eight-Fold Dynasty. Ozone and gunpowder hung heavy in the air, testament to recent gun fire and thorough, rigorous testing of the death dealing arsenal.

S-Pos strutted into the weapons gallery as if he owned the place, beaming with paternal pride at the collection. "Check it out, Johnny. Hell of a toybox, eh brudda?" S-Pos walked over to a pair of Triads, their immaculate black suits marred only by sky-blue Earmuffs hanging about their necks. One was a short fellow with spiky black hair. The other was a dusky lady with a wicked scar over one eye. Johnny knew that whatever made that mark hadn't done it clean. It spoke of spite fueled violence and surviving death by a hair's breadth.

S-Pos waved Johnny back a second, his manic grin never wavering and started up a hushed conference with his two new compatriots. Johnny held back, anxiously looking around the room. *Gotta consult with the rulers of the roost, is that it? Fine, I'll sign whatever waivers they need me too. Not like I haven't already signed away my life. What else can they take?*

At least, all Johnny heard was his garishly clad escort ask, "Yeah, sure, fine, but is it ready?" and the spikey-haired Triad pulled out a reinforced plastic suitcase, the kind that could survive fire, freezing, or flood. S-Pos cracked the lid and reached in with an appreciative laugh.

"Da Pos promises and Da Pos delivers." The boardshort-toting Triad hefted a gleaming pistol and began extolling its many virtues at length. It was one-part tutorial and one-part sales pitch. "This beauty right here is strong enough to make an Auggie think twice about screwing with you and big enough to make your wife love you again. It holds twelve rounds, fits easily into a waistband, and roars louder than your mom when I'm screwing her. Perfect to put anything you need in the ground."

Johnny practically salivated, lost in his revenge fantasies. But even as he reached for the gun, S-Pos put it down.

"But first we gotta make sure you aren't a danger to yourself and others. So we start a little smaller." He handed Johnny a significantly smaller gun and pointed him down range. "Go ahead and line up with the closest victim there. That rusty barrel, the one full of holes. See what you got."

Johnny took a deep breath and sighted down the barrel. *Nothing to worry about. I've handled guns before. Twice. Years ago. Doesn't matter. Just like aiming an old-fashioned mic.*

When he gently squeezed the trigger, things took a turn for the worse. Gently wasn't something Johnny had quite mastered with his new muscles. He jerked on the trigger, pulling the gun down hard and fast. Shocked at the unexpected swerve in his bullet thrower, Johnny compensated. Overcompensated, in fact. The recently enhanced shock-jock jerked the gun up and over his head, finger spasming on the trigger and spewing bullets across the wrong side of the range. Realizing he was spraying bullets all over the place, Johnny dropped the gun in a panic.

For a moment silence reigned. The weapons holder glared up at Johnny from where she'd gone prone on the ground, scarred eye open wide in shock and anger, one hand in her vest, presumably ready to draw her own firearm and end Johnny on the spot. Spiky hair lay sprawled against the wall, frozen stiff. The middle of his gelled hair was simply gone, a stray bullet having dug a deep furrow through the styled mess.

S-Pos stood up from behind a weapons rack, where he'd ducked to with amazing speed. The Triad rep sighed and shook his shaved head. "We got our work cut out for us, brudda."

≈

Months later, Johnny C. Vid, the man, the myth, the legend, sweated under his sleek leather overcoat as he stalked through a grime encrusted tunnel. The thing might be stylish on the street and thick enough to save his guts in a knife fight, but in the city's service tunnels it hung on him like a death sentence.

At least I smell right at home. Deep in the bowels of the Heap, the reeking tunnels gathered all the pungent discards of the world above. Large enough to have a truck pass through them, which often happened as civic workers bypassed the hustle and bustle of the city using the dim pathways, they served as the veins of the sprawling megalopolis. Grease, oil, and other less pleasant remains all found their way down to the byzantine sewer system. *They always did say shit rolled downhill.*

It was here, in this stinking morass of rusting pipes and dripping refuse, that Johnny's quarry waited.

Sweaty palms clung possessively to cold steel. A gift from his recent benefactors. The giant handgun looked oversized in Johnny's wiry hands. Sleek as hell and big enough to make Johnny feel inadequate, the chrome cannon could put a hole in the wall large enough to drive a truck through it. That's the way it was sold to Johnny anyway. He hoped it lived up to its hype.

For what he was hunting he needed something strong enough to put down the devil.

Fingers twitching around the grip, Johnny's sweat had nothing to do with the heat as he remembered his brush with death.

Bone-picker. Rag-man. *Butcher.*

Pressed against a tunnel wall, Johnny grimaced and rolled his shoulders, shaking off phantom pains of a rusty hook digging into meat and bone. Though the Triad chem-heads and body-docs patched him up good as new with bionics and cloned tissue, the phantom pains lingered alongside Johnny's grudge. He'd hung among the pig-faced monster's other victims, flailing like a gutted fish on the end of a line, one more life to be snuffed out for the twisted pleasures of the Butcher.

The thing had been a monster, a nightmare face covered in a pig mask stolen from some rotting pile of trash. Bloated and misshapen with rolling slabs of artificial muscle, the creature dragged his nonsense body through the dark corners of the city-sized trash heap, galvanized rubber apron straining to contain its uneven bulk.

I barely escaped and not even in one piece. Johnny remembered how he had rewired his own brain to stun the monster with a feedback loop. Johnny's eyes and hands twitched in remembered pain, the nerve rending agony lingering like echoes in an empty temple. *Nothing but neurons misfiring and my brain tearing my body apart.* Johnny fought the panic down, smothering it beneath the rage that rose inside him every time he remembered the pig-faced murderer. *Thankfully that bloated sack of shit hurt as much as I did when he tried to jack into my brain.* Even in the dank service tunnels, Johnny still smelt the charnel house smell, the copper tinged rot of the Butcher's lair that filled his nose from being hung like a side of beef to dragging himself across its soiled floor. His vision swimming with pain and blacking out, Johnny had tumbled down an old pneumatic mail chute.

The miles long tubing spat the escapee out, broken, bloody, but breathing.

But the Butcher still lived, still hunted, stealing souls in the Heap. No one noticed. No one cared. This was the Heap. A few more dregs vanished, no one lost any sleep over it. But Johnny cared. Cared enough to make a deal with some very bad people to get back on his feet. Cared enough to hunt the freak through warrens of reeking tunnels and back alley storm drains.

Which brings me here, to this wretched shit-hole. I swore, sitting in that pile of your victims, I'd hunt you down and end you, you pig-faced bastard. I'm going to make my life mine again, starting with your death. I know you're here. I know it. I can taste your insanity.

Even after being released from the Triads tender care, he'd spent months tracking the bastard down but Johnny swore it ended today. The vengeful hunter crouched, doing his best imitation of countless war movies and spy flicks, and listened. A soft tinkle rang out, chains dangling in a muggy breeze, the metal wind chimes of the damned.

Gotcha.

Johnny hurled himself around the corner and unloaded the hand cannon with a snarl and a curse. "Die, you son of a bitch!"

The steel cannon bucked like a living thing, gunshot roaring in the bare room, bullets cratering aged concrete. Johnny emptied the clip before he realized his prey wasn't there. Even as Johnny's valiant cry, worthy of any Storm Lee action flick, died with the echoes of gunshot, the shock-jock knew he'd missed his chance.

No carnival of horrors. No hanging bodies. No bloated monster, living or dead, lay before him.

Only rusting metal hooks and stained concrete floor. Makeshift benches filled with a workshop's worth of barbed wire, vicious blades, and other wicked tools of the monster's trade stood as testament to his sick workmanship. Bits of grisly meat and wine-dark stains remained, legacies of the Butcher's handiwork.

Empty. Just like the others. Johnny lost count of how many bolt holes and lairs he'd uncovered, only to find it deserted. Once more, the Butcher slipped through his grasp.

He swore the sick fucker's chortling laughter hung in the air.

Long ago, Johnny prided himself on his professionalism and cool detachment. Before the pressure of fame and profiting from others' tragedy grew too much, Johnny had gone anywhere and braved anything without batting an eye. He'd made a damn good living by daring where others wouldn't, covering all the gory details of atrocity and horrors for a hungry audience without blinking. J.C. Vid had been legendary for the lengths he'd go to in order to get a scoop.

I was ruthless, hungry. Nothing could stop me. I walked into burning buildings, shadowed private investigators, and jumped right into gunfights. Shook hands with criminals, psychopaths, and even lawyers. All while the camera was rolling. Always came out smiling and the audience loved me for it.

But that was a lifetime ago. Before he'd turned to Vicarious Reality to take the edge off, tumbled down the social ladder until he fell of it into the Heap, and long before he'd survived the Butcher. *I've come a long way from hobnobbing with vid-stars and corporate executives over champagne and caviar.*

Older, wiser, and with a whole lot more to be pissed about, Johnny gave into the rage. Screaming and cursing like a juvie on a playground, the disappointed vengeance seeker kicked over the makeshift tables, sending corrugated steel barrels and foam-frame crates tumbling. Panting, Johnny paced around the room, sucking in deep breaths to calm himself.

Think. Bits are still fresh. He can't have been gone long. Maybe I can find a clue.

Poking around the vacant lair, Johnny put his reawakened investigative journalist talents to work, desperately looking for a clue to his pig-face quarry's location.

Whether through atrophied abilities on Johnny's part or cunning of his enemy, no clue presented itself to the former junkie. With a heavy sigh, Johnny looked around, sat back on his haunches, and mulled over his options.

Another dead end. Now I have to wait until the murderous freak attacks again and track him down.

A high-pitched beeping interrupted the would-be action hero's brooding. Looking down, Johnny saw his scratched and dented wrist-comm beeping a steady signal. Two flashes of red, one gold. The colors of the Heavenly Gate Triads.

His noble benefactors who also currently owned Johnny's sorry ass.

My esteemed masters are jerking my leash. Wonderful. A perfect end to the perfect day.

≈

In most stories, the hero got into their gleaming plas-steel chariot and sped off into the night after a successful quest, tearing off on an endless pursuit of justice. Naturally, Johnny felt a little cheated when he kicked open the service hatch and stepped into hazy daylight filtered through layers of fog and a nagging sense of unfinished business dogged his feet in lieu of triumph.

Furthermore, his chariot was anything but gleaming. It was a tired and worn four-wheeled station wagon, the kind used by burnt-out paper pushers to haul their mewling spawn on vacations and field trips. The clunker sat hunkered at the edge of a chain link fence inside the municipal works compound where Johnny bribed one of the plant workers a handful of creds to ignore it. Picking his way through the tangle of pipes, some broken, some functional, zigging and zagging in a civil engineer's worst nightmare, Johnny shook his head.

The beat-up roadster wasn't even his, on loan from the Heavenly Gate Triads. They didn't like waiting on little things like bus schedules.

And they don't take smelling like a latrine as an excuse for tardiness.

Pulling out his oversized gun, Johnny hesitated before he flicked the safety on and shoved the bulky bullet chucker into the glove box.

He didn't expect to need it where he was going. *It wouldn't do me any good if I did.*

Stinking and tired, Johnny fired up the car with a clattering roar and drove out to meet his esteemed colleagues.

Leaving the industrial parklands and its humming steel, Johnny C. Vid skirted the edge of the Heap, where the half-forgotten urban wasteland brushed against places where people still gave a damn. Turning onto Route 1, the highway's original name lost and redundant, swallowed up by the Heap, Johnny wound his way through a series of high rises and strip malls, stopping to park before his employers' hotel.

Marble columns, chased in rose-red, framed an immaculately clean building front. Crimson and gold framed each window, rising up, up, up in shining splendor. It towered as a beacon of wealth and comfort, in contrast to the dimly lit cracked tenements and corrugated metal sheds visible across the freeway.

Carmine suited guards stood at crisp attention, the only creases in their suits created by their gun holsters and straps. They watched everything, heads turning unceasingly, sunglasses linked to any number of tastefully concealed targeting arrays. Each one of the guards bore the symbol of the Heavenly Gate Triads, three vertical golden bars on a field of crimson.

That same symbol stood proudly on the front doors of the Gentle Fields Hotel.

In more polite areas, the criminal underbelly had to be subtle. The Empress did not abide open challenges to her rule. Here in the Heap, where the criminal element was more of an overbelly, the Triads didn't have to hide. They were practically the local government.

No one cares if the animals kill each other, right?

A polite cough from the valet kicked Johnny into gear. He realized he'd been sitting in the car, gripping the wheel with white knuckled force. A kind observation might call it procrastination. A more honest one would call it hiding.

Time to bite the bullet and get this over with. I've survived worse. As he slid from the peeling pleather seat and handed over the keys, Johnny desperately tried to convince himself that was true.

The guards greeted the filthy hunter at the door, far too polite and courteous to mention Johnny smelled like he'd spent the day stalking through a sewer. Which, of course, he had.

That's customer service with the Triads for you. All smiles until they beat the crap out of you. The message was clear to Johnny. For now, he retained favor with the boss. Play nice or lose your teeth.

Deciding he liked his pearly whites where they were, Johnny nodded back and made idle chit chat. Everyone was all smiles as they led him through the grandiose lobby. Even the pretty receptionists behind the desk, all ludicrously good looking young men and women, smiled the whole time, practically glowing under the mammoth chandelier's golden light.

The tasteful décor and politeness continued into a private meeting room where Johnny came face to face with Hoa Dang. A well-fed man whose artificially smooth complexion spoke of endless rejuvenat treatments and the very best clean living that money could buy. He seemed like the kindly uncle you could tell your problems too and be the very best bad influence you could hope for on your kids. It made Johnny a little sorry he'd tracked sewer muck onto Hoa Dang's clean carpets.

The fact that Hoa Dang could order his death as easily as a martini made the former shock-jock a bit sorrier about the ruined gold and crimson cloth.

Despite his easy smile, Hoa Dang was an inordinately dangerous man. That he owned Johnny lock, stock, and barrel only compounded matters.

The arrangement stung even more, since Johnny had come to him.

Johnny had been making a deal with one devil to kill another. Sitting in that worn hospital bed, Johnny knew he couldn't wait for the long rehabilitative recovery, couldn't even hope to afford it, so the survivor asked all the wrong people for help.

Hell, I practically begged them to let me sign my life away. Good thing Elder Dang was a "fan" from my shock-jock days.

A bit of haggling, aided by the last bit of his tarnished fame and a bargain was struck. Extensive drug therapy and cybernetic bracing brought his body to peak condition and they'd even upgraded his slagged cyber-jack as a freebie. Johnny felt healthier than ever.

Once whole, Johnny C. Vid raced back out onto the streets, an Ahab seeking his demon-whale. But the shock-jock's hunt dragged on and on, full of dead ends and wrong turns. The Triads didn't mind his hobby, so long as it didn't interfere with work.

I swore I'd sell my soul for revenge. Now it's time to give the devil his due.

"Mr. Vid!" Hoa Dang always called him by his shock-jock handle, even claimed he was a "big fan" of Johnny's old work. Eldear Dang's fan mail from Johnny's heyday as a net star was the reason Johnny thought to reach out in the first place. "Thank you for coming on such short notice."

"Of course, Elder Dang. I'd never be so impolite to refuse a meeting with so respected a figure as yourself." Johnny remembered when he used to ask the hard hitting questions of dangerous men like Dang. Now, here he was bowing and scraping. *Sucking up? Maybe a little. But observing the niceties never got anyone killed.*

The crime boss chuckled warmly and waved for Johnny to sit down, who did so with a squish as his soiled trench coat met plush seat. Chuckles erupted into open guffaws. Hoa Dang shook his head.

"Ah, Johnny. Still chasing your phantom, I see."

"The Butcher is real, Honored Elder. I have the scars to prove it."

Hoa Dang nodded sagely. "Indeed, it is our wet-ware that covers those scars. You have lived an interesting life. And it is just that lifetime of skills I would like to utilize."

The Triad crime boss took a brief drink of amber liquid from a crystal cup before continuing. "Our operations have experience certain interruptions. It isn't merely supplies going missing. Such troubles could be resolved with a bit of personnel turnover."

It took all of Johnny's old interviewer skills not to balk. *Wow, that is a hell of euphemism for shooting whoever fucked up in the head.*

Johnny kept his expression carefully neutral as Dang continued. "In fact, when we went to speak to our trusted subordinates, we found them gone as well, leaving no trace. They have not fled with ill-gotten goods. Urgent inquiries prove they have not been so unwise. They have simply disappeared. Our staff is vanishing at an alarming rate. None of our competitors are claiming responsibility or making a move on us."

"While I sympathize for your troubles, Elder Dang, how may my skills assist?"

The crime boss' paternal smile did nothing to reassure the sewer slime covered Mr. Vid. "Our agents are well known to our competitors. Like family, really. We do not wish to tip our hand that something is wrong. So we would like you to make some interviews on our behalf. You used to do those rather often, I understand."

Johnny felt a little relieved they didn't want him to do wetwork. It let him pretend his hands were clean. Not that he expected them to call on ol' J.C. Vid to snuff anyone out. The Triads had their own hit crews for that, literal killing machines more cyber-ware than flesh. Besides, the Heavenly Gate members didn't trust him around fire arms since the firing range incident. Johnny didn't blame them. *So I was a little off with my aim! Tetsuo's hair will grow back, it was just a graze. I slung cameras and microphones, not firearms, for pity's sake. When I shot people they got recorded. They didn't get dead.*

"I am flattered Elder Dang, but are you certain it would be wise to send me. I am a bit of a celebrity figure." Feeble excuse, true, but Johnny wasn't above trying it.

A shadow crossed Hoa Dang's face, something that said he knew exactly what the burnout's game was. "Memories fade rather quickly, Mr. Vid. You are not so infamous now as you would like to think."

Translation: Nice try. *Shit. Swing and a miss.*

"As you say, Honored Elder. I bow to your superior wisdom."

A cruel twinkle replaced the shadow upon the don's face. "In doing so, you display wisdom yourself." He nodded to his guards. "You see? I knew my third wife was right about him." The large man turned back to Johnny. "With proper training, we just might civilize you."

Hoa Dang let out another belly laugh and everyone joined in at the shock-jock's expense, who gritted his teeth in what might have passed as a smile.

After all, it didn't hurt to be polite.

Johnny's rictus grin stayed in place until the valet brought the loaner to the front of the casino and he'd driven the clunker around the corner. It fell from the shock-jock's face as he leaned back, body shaking with tension.

What a rush. Can't wait to do that never. The Triad gangs had always been the bogeymen in Mr. Vid's half-life as a burnout on the streets. Cross them and you disappeared. They might as well have been gods half the time, their names invoked as protection or curse.

Now I'm running errands on behalf of the head of the Heavenly Gate Triads.

Johnny's mind flashed to when he'd limped into the free clinic, beaten, bloody, and barely alive. He'd taken his place in line with the other dregs and burnouts. The staff took one look at him, marked their charts, and moved on. Life was cheap in the Heap and he was nothing they hadn't seen before.

Invisible, even when he was dying.

Guess I'm moving up in the world.

Somehow, the thought failed to cheer Johnny up.

CHAPTER 5:
ABSENT FRIENDS

In THE HEAP, asking after somebody's business usually meant a quick and unfortunate end. Fortunately, Johnny learned long ago how to ask the right questions and who to ask them to.

Which in Johnny's case meant the dregs and the forgotten, the ones who dropped off the face of the planet. The street folk of the Heap were among the lowest of the low, barely even pawns in the endless struggles and turf wars between gangs and rarely worth bothering for press-ganged labor by sleazy corporations.

Johnny knew all this because he'd been one of them before he'd become a Triad gopher. A burnout. A loser. Invisible. Which was just perfect for hearing things others didn't want you to hear. With a little hard coin, because credits didn't buy a damn thing from the wrong kinds of people, Johnny learned everything the street people could know.

Which sometimes meant learning jack shit.

"Really, Pang? Nothing? The Phoenix Band, Red Hatchets, and Pure Lotus Boys? No one's making any moves on rival gangs?"

The shaggy vagrant across from him, more grime than skin, shook his head weakly, greasy hair waving like damp seaweed. Despite his disheveled appearance, Johnny considered Pang an honest friend, a rare thing in the Heap. Pang had stood by Johnny when the shock-jock had been a new fish on the streets, taught the VR addict how to live in the chrome and neon megapolis. Without Pang, Johnny wouldn't have survived his first year in the urban wasteland. Pang still talked to Johnny, even though the former shock-jock wore the colors of the Heavenly Gate and ran around at a crime bosses' beck and call. Street folks generally stayed off of the radar of the organized syndicates. Healthier that way.

Pang gave a phlegmatic shrug. "Nope. Not a damn one. Something's got the families spooked but no one's moving on the others. Not even the murder-clades are drawing steel. I hear tales though..."

Johnny waited a moment too long and the street beggar rolled rheumy eyes and shook his bowl with a meaningful grunt. Once a few coins filled it, the raspy voice continued.

"Everyone's been on guard. Isn't just the big names. Little fish been freaking out too. Streets ain't safe at night."

"They never were."

Johnny's profound statement of the obvious earned a nod from the disheveled hobo. "Damn straight, but it's gotten worse lately. People been vanishing. All sorts. Cooks, peddlers, tailors, and chop-shop docs. No rhyme or reason to it. The gangs, well, you understood 'em. They kill you and let folks know who dunnit and why. Unless its family business, then you keep it in the family. This time, no one's saying shit. Folks are talking, though."

"Talking 'bout what?"

Another grunt from the Beggar and more coins magically appeared in Pang's begging bowl. "Come on, you old bastard. Talking about what?"

"Things. People been seein' things. Things that ain't right. Moving in the shadows. Like man-shapes but wrong. Weird animal faces. Dragging people off in sacks."

Johnny's blood ran cold. "Sacks?"

"Huge things. Large enough to stuff a person in. Says they hear rattling, like chains of the damned."

"That pig-faced bastard. I nailed him. Thanks, Pang!" Johnny hurled a few more coins at the beggar and shuffled off to make a call. He didn't even hear Pang's confused muttering.

"He knew about the piggy man? Hope he knows about the other masks."

≈

As soon as Johnny was a reasonably safe distance from Pang and the other street folk's prying ears, he placed a call to Elder Dang. Given Johnny's newfound status with the Triad syndicate, it was highly unlikely anyone would mess with the shock-jock in this corner of the Heap. Still, Johnny had found in his long and colorful career that it didn't hurt to cover your bases. He'd made more than one big scoop thanks to some street punk's loose lips and had traded ganger gossip for a warm bed and a warmer hit of VR in his days on the streets. Information wasn't power to Pang and his ilk, it was their life's blood, worth more than any cold hard cash. The street folk lived and died by what they knew. Any bit of gossip might be embarrassing for Elder Dang and the Heavenly Gates. And that meant somebody died.

Johnny paced impatiently as he tried to contact his current boss. The communicator beeped more than a few times before Hoa Dang answered. Excited as he was, Johnny still minded his manners. "Honored Elder, I hope I did not catch you an inauspicious time."

The flushed faced Mafioso grinned ear to ear. "Mr. Vid! How good of you to call! So soon, as well. You have exceeded our expectations."

Formalities out of the way, the excited shock-jock spilled the whole story. "It's him, Hoa Dang. The pig-faced bastard. The Butcher's been taking folks from all around, dragging them off to gods know where. He's why your people have been vanishing."

"Mr. Vid..."

"I'm so close! This time, his ass is mine."

"Mr. Vid!"

Johnny swallowed his words as the crime lord's displeased voice cracked like a whip. "We tasked you to inquire after our missing personnel and any who might have attacked us. You disappoint us with fairy-tales."

"Honored Elder, please."

"No!" The Triad boss' cold snarl cut Johnny off with the finality of a brick wall. "You allow your personal vendetta to cloud your mind. We demand answers for our own woes, solid evidence, not more of your meaningless shadow chase. You owe the Heavenly Gate, Mr. Vid. We would see that debt repaid. In service. Or in blood. Call with solid evidence or do not call at all."

Johnny returned to his car and slumped morosely into the worn seat, hands shaking once again.

This time it wasn't just nerves. *Dammit, I've been clean for months. Why now?*

But deep down, Johnny knew why. He'd been plumbing around his old haunts, the fake-life dives and VR pits he used to frequent, looking for answers from the dregs and burnouts, the easiest victims of the Butcher. Like an alcoholic going back to a bar, old hungers reawakened. It didn't help that the dreams never stopped.

Calm down. You beat it before. You aren't that junkie anymore. It took a great many more breathes to stop the shakes. *I still need to convince Hoa Dang to let me off the hook.*

Johnny racked his brain for some sort of a solution to his quandary. Not that he had much experience with placating an incredibly powerful and terrifying crime boss.

But I'm no stranger to terrifying bosses. Theresa was at least as scary Elder Dang. She'd have given me the axe for real if she could have.

Reflection on the spectacular ending of his shock-jock career sparked an idea in Johnny's overtaxed brain. A grin spread onto Mr. Vid's face. It felt odd to him. He hadn't had cause to smile in some time.

If a trip down memory lane to the bad old days didn't work, let's try the worse old days.

≈

Johnny C. Vid adjusted his tie for the fifth time in as many minutes. His reflection in the restroom mirror looked as shitty as he felt. A dapper dead man walking. A corpse in corporate chic. What used to feel like a second skin to him felt more like a special fitted coffin. Johnny's hands shook with nerves.

What he hoped was nerves.

Johnny looked his mirror self in the eyes and summoned up his courage. *I can do this. I've escaped bloodthirsty serial killers, stared down Triad crime bosses, and even lived through rush hour in the Fast Lanes on Route 1!*

But none those were part of Johnny's old life, his career days. It took everything the former vid-jock had not to run out of the clean and shining Public Eye Media building and go back to the streets. *Except that isn't an option right now. I'd be better off eating a bullet now and saving time.* If Johnny wanted to live long enough to bury the Butcher, he had to go through with this. There were no other options. Splashing water on his face, Johnny plastered on his best broadcast smile and stepped out into the lobby.

Public Eye. One of the largest public entertainment and news conglomerates this side of the Heap. My old employer. Shot a lot of vid-casts for them and ran a lot of miles ambulance chasing. Lotta good times. Johnny shuddered as dead children's eyes, glassy and unseeing, rose in his mind. *Lotta bad as well. I haven't been here since I gave them notice.*

The sterile lobby, gleaming steel and imitation-wood polished to a reflective sheen, brought back a complex net of memories. The Eye were one of the biggest entertainment and news businesses in this corner of the Eight-Fold System and it showed in their Kadath office. *Basic Corporate Psychology; if you got it, flaunt it. I lived by that. I was one of their best. Until it all became too much and the VR took over.*

Now here Johnny was, trying to trade on the ashes of any good faith left after he'd burned his bridges for good.

At least Candace is still willing to see me. Now if only I can avoid Theresa. Ms. Theresa Nguyen, his old boss, had made it abundantly clear that Johnny C. Vid was not welcome back at the Public Eye. If she found him, his ass was grass, along with any chance of finding a lead on what was going on in the Heap. *If my connections in low places didn't work, it's time to try official channels.*

Stepping into the elevator, Johnny rode the gleaming box skyward to say hello to an old friend. Up and up he went, strolling out of the elevator onto plush carpet. Soft music played and a slight smell of jasmine, iris, and violet lingered in the air. All designed to welcome visitors and put them at ease. Unlike the dreary and sterile concrete box Johnny'd been living in, the place actually cared about making a good impression.

Yeah, because here, unlike with the Triads, you actually expect visitors and its impolite to show off your guns until after the contract is signed.

With a gentle knock on the door, Johnny walked in to meet an old friend.

"Johnny C. Vid! Back from the dead!" Candace's infectious grin thawed Johnny's forced death mask into a real smile. Candace Blythe's piercing dark eyes remained sharp as ever as she brushed half of a brilliantly dyed red mohawk out from in front of them. "Good to see you, buddy."

"You too, Candace." Johnny meant every word. Though he'd willingly left most of his former life behind, Candace was one of the few pieces of it that he missed. First a rival, then partner in crime, Candace and Johnny had navigated the treacherous peaks and valleys of office politics at the Public Eye.

Johnny sat and down and the two shock-jocks caught up and chatted about nothing much, easily slipping into old routines. Gripes and grievances about management, the economy, and whatever else they felt like bitching about were the topic du jour. For a moment, Johnny felt at ease, all the horrors plaguing his life melting away. Only a moment but it was something.

"So, what brings you to my humble domain?" The well-groomed shock-jock gave an utterly hollow self-deprecating wave at her private office, covered in a layer of reminders, holo-notes, and barely organized chaos.

"I need some info." *Better lay all the cards on the table. Candace always could tell when I'm lying.*

The esteemed Ms. Blythe frowned, idly flicking her hanging crimson Mohawk. "Come on, J.C. You know I can't give scoops out to rival news companies."

Johnny shook his head. "I'm not working for the competition."

Her eyebrows shot up in surprise before drawing down into an angry arrow point. "You went Incorporated? Damn, that takes some balls. Double no-go, amigo. I have met the enemy and he is you!"

Johnny held up his hands defensively as the dagger like nail pointed accusingly at him. "Nothing like that. I'm out of the biz. This is personal."

Candace's fingers started drumming on the faux-oak desk. "I won't help you score another fix."

"I'm not a damn junkie! I don't need a fix!"

"Then why have your hands been shaking this whole time?"

Johnny looked down to stare at his traitorous hands. They jigged in an anxious dance on the arm rests. Seemed they'd been doing that for a while.

Johnny clamped his hands down on his knees and looked away for a moment. When he turned back to his old friend, Johnny's hands and volume were only barely held in place by a supreme effort of self-control.

"I'm not a junkie. Not anymore. I just want to know if you've heard anything about thing going down in the Heap."

Candace snorted loudly. "The Heap? J.C., maybe you forgot, but we follow news here at the Eye. We watch everything that matters. Which naturally precludes that trash-pile. Who cares what happens to a bunch of nobodies?"

Face flushed, Johnny looked at his still jittering hands. "I was one of those nobodies."

"I can't help you." Candace spoke the refusal softly, almost kindly, but it was still a refusal.

"Can't or won't?" Even as he snapped, Johnny knew he'd stepped in it.

All trace of softness vanished from Candace's face as she glared at her old partner. "Do I hear an echo? I remember you mouthing off to Theresa like that when she refused you some leave time to indulge your godsdamned habit! It's that sort of attitude that got your ass thrown out into the street."

"I left on my own!"

"To avoid the axe, you fucking coward!"

Johnny looked down, unable to meet her gaze again. *Dammit, she's right. I ran. Wanted to have something on my terms.*

She glared at him in silence before turning to her computer. "Thanks for the visit, pal. You know the way out. Go back to those nobodies you care so much about. Get yourself another fix."

Johnny got up and quietly walked out the door. He didn't utter a word as he walked through the plush and sweet-smelling hallway. His face might have been a mask for all the emotion it showed when he pushed the button and stepped into the elevator.

Only once the doors slid shut did Johnny start to scream.

He punched the wall again and again, hurling himself around the gleaming box like a lunatic in an asylum until he'd calmed down. Johnny cradled his throbbing hands and snarled quietly. There was one person left he could go to. The only other person alive who knew about the Butcher.

Smiler.

If I can find the little shit, I can make him talk.

Johnny looked down at his shaking hands, bruised and bloody.

Maybe score a hit. Just one. For old time's sake.

≈

It didn't take long to ferret out his old supplier's whereabouts. Unsurprisingly, the grinning turd wasn't well loved in the Heap. A few credits and the VR burnouts gave up his hiding hole in no time flat.

Damn. Never can trust a junkie.

Turned out Smiler's lair was the same building Johnny squatted in as he dodged his miserable life by vicariously living through others. It seemed fitting they'd come full circle.

Least I'm better dressed this time. Horribly out of place in the business suit he'd met Candace in, the weight of his hand cannon rested comfortably in Johnny's grip. Normally not the kind of guy to flaunt hardware, Johnny figured it should deter the street toughs and scam-hands looking for an easy mark. Besides, it might be necessary to jog Smiler's memory about the Butcher.

Stomping noisily through the old tenements, Johnny called out to his former supplier.

"Smiler? Come on out, buddy. It's your old pal, Johnny C. Vid." His voice echoed weirdly in the derelict flats, sounding back like the ghost of his shock-jock days. No reply except the hum of overtaxed fans. Not too surprising given the last time they'd met Johnny strangled the snaggle-toothed bastard within an inch of his life. The other tenants had either already fled or were laying low. Sticking your neck out was a good way to lose your head in the Heap.

"Surely you wouldn't let a few death threats get between friends? I mean, come on, some people pay good credits for that sort of hands on action." Still nothing. *Fine, time for a different tactic.* "Okay, you little shit, let's make this simple. You come out and play and not only will I not cut your balls off and feed them to you, I promise to hook you up with the Triads."

The shock-jock heard a creak from further into the tenement and crept forward, until he stopped in front of an ancient door, more rust than metal. "Heeerrreee's Johnny!"

As he shouldered the rust patched door open with a grunt, Johnny's next clever quip died in his throat.

He'd found Smiler.

Strung up with vicious barbed wire like a festive turkey, the bottom feeder had been flayed open from throat to groin, skin peeled back to reveal glistening viscera within. Flies buzzed about the room, laying eggs in the festering shit of Smiler's earthly remains. The drug peddler's mouth hung open in a frozen scream, his customary sickly grin utterly wiped away in a rictus of pain. Pieces of Smiler's liver were crammed into his mouth, glistening like an arterial apple in a roast pig.

Turning into the hall, Johnny puked until his stomach was empty, dry heaves wracking his body.

It was a sad truth that Mr. Vid was no stranger to violence. He'd seen his share of horrors in his career with the Public Eye, which only made Smiler's death hit harder. All the memories Johnny had been running from, the battlefields, hell-pits, and massacres, came rushing back, his nightmares manifested in gruesome clarity.

Guess I can't make good on my threat. Someone beat me to it. Damn. So much for that fix.

Except, as he rocked back and forth struggling through the old pain, Johnny realized an absence of the newly returned cravings, replaced by a now familiar warmth. Rage and hate churned in his guts instead of disgust, warming him like fire. The same all-consuming fire that burned when he'd clawed his way out of the Boneyard and made him deal with the very dangerous men and women of the Triads. No surprise, really. Johnny recognized the handiwork on Smiler.

That son of a bitch. The Butcher left me a calling card. Letting me know I'm not just hunting him, he's hunting me. How did the sick bastard know who I was? The options were numerous, from torturing it out of Smiler, finding his cred-card, or just recognizing Johnny's face from long faded glory days on the vid-feed. A last, more terrifying option hit Johnny like an icicle in the gut. The monster could have snatched bits of his life from the feedback loop when they connected.

That monster could have ripped information from all that static noise.

Johnny shuddered at the thought of how much will and focus it would take to push through the backlash long enough to snatch some sense of the garbled impressions.

Suspicion, followed by horror, flooded through Johnny as his brain connected the pieces. He frantically pulled up the list of the vanished Triads. Names flashed, a death march in unassuming font and gentle backlighting. Chu Shi, Greg B. Goody, even Old Man Shen.

All low level goons, local Triad help. All folks Johnny knew.

The chem-heads and cyber-docs who fixed my body, the faces and contacts who kept me caught up when I came outta the bunker, even that nice street tailor who hooked me up with new threads. That monster is killing folks I know. Johnny's head cocked, like a dog listening to a far off sound. *But he couldn't have plucked it out of our brain-scramble, I met them after I escaped. Which means the beast's been stalking me.*

The ex-junkie wracked his brain, trying to dredge up who could be next on the chopping block.

Unless the sick bastard is chasing down fast food workers and synth-coffee slingers I've bought food from, no one is left. I don't talk to anyone these days except beggars and Triad crime bosses.

A flash of red hair popped into Mr. Vid's mind and it took everything he had not to throw up again.

Oh gods. Candace.

Running from the grisly murder scene, Johnny pulled up Candace's number, desperately trying to warn his old friend. He got nothing but a polite recording for his efforts.

I know I was an ass, Candace, but this is no time to screen your calls!

As he slammed into his seat, Johnny kicked the car into gear and tore off into the streets in a cloud of oily exhaust, racing the setting sun.

The front end of Johnny's junker bounced off the curb as he screeched to a halt in front of the Public Eye offices. Law abiding citizenry, out for an unconcerned evening stroll in their finery, sniffed and pointedly looked away, far too polite to express their disapproval more directly. Ducking out his car, the frenzied former employee shoved the mirrored glass doors open. "Call Ms. Blythe, now!"

A cold and empty silence greeted Johnny's panicked shout. *Not a good sign. Maybe the guard has the night off. Maybe they're on their night rounds. Maybe.*

Johnny ran to the elevators, one hand shoved into his suit's vest, desperately clutching his gun as he hammered on the up button with his free hand. Cursing soundly at the elevator's leisurely pace,

Johnny took to the stairs. Wheezing, panting, and utterly grateful for the Triad enhancements that made up for actual training, Johnny slammed his winded frame into Candace's office.

"Let her go, you monster!"

Candace Blythe looked up at her old friend barging in with wide eyes. Alone. In her office. Perfectly fine. "Johnny? What in the nine hundred names of god are you doing?"

Johnny froze, eyes darting about the room, trying to find a clear and precise way to rationalize kicking down the door with gun drawn while screaming about monsters. "Uhhh." The potted plants did not provide an adequate answer to Johnny's conundrum.

She stared coldly at her former co-worker. "When I told you to 'get a fix,' I didn't mean come back and share."

Johnny stuffed the gun behind his back, like a child caught filching sweets. "No, Candy, please, you-gotta-listen-to-me." Panic blurred his words together but Candace got the gist of desperate pleading easily enough.

"I don't have to do anything of the sort, J.C. And you lost the right to call me that a long time ago. Hated the stupid nickname back then, too." Muttering darkly, Blythe opened a line to the front desk from her desk-comp. She could have sub-voxed it, sent an emergency impulse via the cyber-comms, but

Candace was making a point. She wanted Johnny to see her do it. Johnny's old working buddy was done putting up with his shit. "Laura, could you come up and escort an old friend out of the building?" Only the eerie silence of the lobby poured through the open line. "Laura, you there?" Her red brows furrowed as she glared at the anxiously pacing Johnny. "What did you do?"

"Nothing! No one was downstairs when I got here. Lights are off, nobody's home."

"It's the graveyard shift, Johnny. Of course the place is dead."

Johnny winced at her word choice. "I'm trying to tell you, you're in danger."

"Yeah, from an old friend waving a gun around while fried out of his mind."

"Dammit, for the last time, I'm not on anything! There is a monster! He's coming here to kill you."

Even as he rambled, Johnny realized he wasn't helping his case. *Oh, godsdammit.*

"Monster. Right, uh-huh, gotcha."

"Look, Candace, I'm begging you, we have to leave, and we have to leave now."

She glared at him a moment, then sat down and calmly steepled her fingers. "You have five minutes to convince me."

"Candace, please."

"Five. Or I call the cops right now."

Johnny sighed and started the whole sad story, right from the beginning. "So there I was, the man, the myth, the legend..."

CHAPTER 6:
DEBTS EARNED
AND DEBTS PAID

AFTER JOHNNY FINISHED one massively truncated story of his escapades, one eye nervously watching the open door of the office, Candace Blythe leaned back with a low whistle. "That is one hell of a trip."

"Candace..."

"Come off it, Johnny! A pig-masked serial killer? And you called him the Butcher? What cheap gore-flick did your fragged mind rip that one from?"

"It seemed to fit. I didn't know what else to call him. We didn't exactly swap business cards." Johnny mumbled sulkily.

"Look, Johnny, I know you believe it, but if you expect me to buy..." Ms. Blythe's lecture came to an abrupt end as the lights cut out. Simultaneous curses made a counterpointed duet in the darkness, one irritated, the other fearful.

A beam of light cut through the dark as Blythe activated the high beam function in her comm. It revealed Johnny crouched low, using a fake potted plant as a sad excuse for cover, eyes wide.

"Not funny, J.C."

But the shock-jock wasn't listening. He was too busy spinning in circles, trying to watch everywhere at once like a frightened animal. "He's here." Johnny hissed through gritted teeth. Candace watched the trembling gun dart about with worried eyes.

Seconds ticked by and both of them looked toward to the open door, a portal of darkness outlined by the soft green glow of emergency lights. That's when the ceiling crashed in on them.

Johnny whirled around even as dust and debris pelted him. The shock-jock coughed and spat out a mouthful of drywall and ferro-crete powder, feverishly rubbing the grime from his eyes. For a moment, Johnny froze as the creature of his nightmares loomed before him in the dim green light. The same stitched pig mask, bloated musculature, and galvanized rubber smock. This time though, it wasn't after Johnny. Not directly. It picked a different victim. The

Butcher had Candace pinned to her desk, oversized hand clamped around her throat.

Johnny screamed. Screamed loud and hard without any of the macho posturing of the action flicks he'd avidly imbibed as a VR addict. His finger twitched rapidly, emptying the clip into the looming beast.

Bullets hammered into the desk, the walls, and even the fake decorative plants but not a one hit the Butcher, who lazily regarded Mr. Vid with a baleful eye, ruined throat letting loose a mocking chortle.

The Triads were right. I can't shoot for shit.

Fortunately, Johnny's dismal accuracy did have one upside. The monster forgot about Candace Blythe. Never a wise decision, in Johnny's experience.

The erstwhile victim flexed her hand, nails extending with a hydraulic *snicht*, before slamming the tips into the Butcher's forearm, hidden needles venting their payloads. The pig-faced bastard roared, lifting her from the desk in his meaty paw before toxin-weakened muscles dropped the mohawked woman.

Johnny and Candace ran from office, the squealing sadist thundering through the debris behind them. Even as the two darted through the darkened corridors, the Butcher tore after them, staggering drunkenly and screaming like the damned.

Unwilling to let his prey escape, the bestial killer let fly with a tarnished hook which missed its mark by inches and thus spared Johnny a repeat performance of his brutal fishhooking during their first meeting.

Thwarted squeals followed Johnny and Candace as they flew down the stair way, followed shortly by the doorway, torn off of its hinges by the Butcher's rage. It narrowly missed crushing Candace's head as it careened and tumbled down the stairwell in a thunderous cacophony. The two shock-jocks never stopped running until they cleared the front doors. Piling into Johnny's car, the survivors made their escape in a howl of smoking tires.

Ensconced in the dubious safety of the rusted junker, Blythe examined her shaking nails with a wry grin. "Enough tranquilizer to put down a splatterball team and the big bastard still kept coming. Damn, I want whatever that guy is on."

Johnny, focus rather diverted between dodging traffic and watching for the persistent Butcher, uttered a quizzical grunt by way of reply.

Candace tapped the side of her nose. "You can't smell it? That chemical tang? He's all hopped up on something. 'Lotta somethings actually.'" She sighed. "Also, hate to say it, but you're right. Butcher works."

Johnny snarled and honked loudly as he swerved around a slow-moving big rig. "Damn, if only we had a camera, I'd go right to the Triads, prove to them the bastard is real."

"Good thing we got one, right here."

"What?" Johnny looked at his crimson haired companion, who tapped one now normal nail to her temple, grinning like the proverbial cat who ate the equally proverbial canary.

"Eye cameras, Johnny boy. Easier to get a scoop when they don't know they're being filmed."

"Never figured you for the implant type, Candace."

"Bite me, J.C. Now, let's go talk to your keepers, shall we? You've got a bogeyman to catch."

≈

"Mr. Vid. You have brought a guest into my home." Hoa Dang, head of the Heavenly Gates Triads left the unspoken "*uninvited*" hanging in the air. Nevertheless, the host of armed and glowering goons surrounding Johnny and Candace effectively communicated Elder Dang's displeasure.

Despite the ire of one of the most dangerous men in the Heap focused on her, Candace Blythe never missed a beat as she extended her hand, as formal and polite as if she was in her office.

"Candace Blythe, Public Eye. Pleased to finally make your acquaintance, Elder Dang. You are a hard man to get a hold of. I've tried to schedule an interview several times." Candace's grin was blinding, augmented pearly whites on display. The grin showed no trace that she and her former co-worker had just escaped a masked serial killer and now stood surrounded by gun toting mobsters.

No stranger to bold moves or paparazzi ambushes, Elder Dang matched Candace with a firm handshake.

"The pleasure is mine, Ms. Blythe. I enjoy your casts for the Eye, though I'll offer no apologies for avoiding being in them. I am a private person by choice. What could be so important that you would come to me after my...polite refusals to your comrades?"

Johnny barely covered a wince at Elder Dang's oblique reference to the Triad response to pushy newscasters. *Poor Yey. He might have been a jerk but I hope he wakes up from the coma one day.*

The implicit threat of life-altering physical violence didn't so much as stir Candace's red mohawk. She carefully drew her comms unit out from her suit, holding it out to the mafioso. "Tell me, Elder Dang, do you like ghost stories?"

Without waiting for a reply, Candace pulled up the recording from her internal camera, blaring the Butcher in all his wretched glory through her comm. Even without the full sensory immersion of VR, the Butcher's malice and hate poured through perfectly clear. More than one of the Triad guards instinctively went for their weapons, jerking back from the miniature horror film.

Even Elder Dang reacted to the video, a raised eyebrow and a sharp triple clap in appreciation of the cheap shock-jock theatrics. *He really is a fan.*

"It seems there is some validity to our esteemed Mr. Vid's tales of a pig-masked killer after all. Though I am appreciative to know my dear friend isn't plagued by hallucinations, why come here?"

"Because you have a vested interest. With what our boy's given me, I've tracked down the Butcher's habits, I can help you find him, and, what's more, I can prove that he's been the one picking off your personnel."

Elder Dang eyes slid from Candace to Johnny C like blade drawn across a whetstone. "You have formidable resources, Ms. Blythe, to know such things."

Johnny couldn't decide whether to smirk or frown. *Bastard. I've showed you the charts and the numbers, tracking the bloody trails of the Butcher's work. Couldn't listen to it coming from me, though, could you? Maybe you'll listen to Candace.*

Truthfully, both shock-jocks were counting on it. They'd planned out their strategy on the ride over and judged it best that Candace take the helm. Elder Dang had heard Johnny's rants about the Butcher too many times to care. *I'm the boy who cried "deranged serial killer." I'd be dismissed as so much wasted air.*

The warning coming from Candace gave the Butcher real weight. And that would make the crime boss sit up and take notice. Elder Dang could not show weakness. His position in the Triad hierarchy meant an air of impeccable competence and ruthlessness. Missing the chance to hunt the beast that had been taking his people for months when it was right in front of him would certainly count as weakness.

Candace picked the thread up smooth as you please. "Thank you, Elder Dang. It's nice to have one's talents recognized." She tossed a wink at Johnny whose waffling smirk toppled firmly onto the frown side of things at Candace's little victory lap.

Thanks for rubbing it in, Candace, old buddy, old pal, old friend.

"Indeed. Though I must ask, what is your...vested interest in this matter?"

The red-headed shock-jock stood stiff backed, a fighter with injured pride. "The Butcher is a monster. He's killed, tortured, and maimed innocent people. He even attacked me and wrecked my office." There was no mistaking which trespass Ms. Blythe found more offensive. "I want to see him dead. For the good of the people, of course."

"Of course. And your price for this invaluable information?"

Candace let loose one of her signature broadcast smiles. "I'm so glad you asked."

The negotiations went smoothly after that. They'd retired to Elder Dang's office for drinks to discuss matters further. The chair Johnny had sat in after his return from the sewers had been replaced entirely. Johnny watched in awe as Candace haggled and schmoozed with Hoa Dang. Despite facing down a Triad family head in his own house, Ms. Blythe didn't yield an inch. Back and forth, point for point they went. Granted, most of the concessions were illusory, as Elder Dang held all the power and could choose to honor or dismiss any agreement made.

In some ways that makes Candace keeping pace all the more impressive.

"In honor of your noble and puissant actions, you shall have an exclusive interview, once matters are handled."

"Very gracious of you, Elder."

They clinked glasses to solidify the deal. Candace turned to Johnny. "Some of us still got it, J.C."

Johnny sipped his drink to cover his gaping mouth. And block any ungracious whining.

Candace celebrated her companion's discomfort only a moment longer than necessary before she cut to the heart of the matter, waving her rice-wine filled glass with gusto. "Well gentleman, this is all well and good, but now to brass tacks. How are we going to catch the beast?"

"I will not send my men chasing shadows. My troops are the best in the Heap but they are unsubtle tools and more likely to drive the creature underground. Besides, it will communicate the wrong message to the other Triads and would risk unnecessary bloodshed." The crime boss turned to his minion with a frown. "Mr. Vid, we expected you to have handled this by now."

Johnny sighed in frustration. "I've tried hunting the bastard down. Each time I find his lair, he's ran off. Always one step ahead. Now it looks like he's been stalking me while I hunted him."

The three fell to silence, each lost in their own heads, until Elder Dang huffed loudly. "Look at you two. So much for the fabled shock-jock's sharp wit. Where are the daring and cunning souls who escaped the Bangkok Quarter and emerged from the Pit of Black Jade unscathed? It is amazing you evaded the Butcher's knives once, much less a second time."

Johnny's head snapped upright, the Triad crime lord's scathing remark firing exhausted neurons. "That's it. He's after me. The Butcher's been stalking me, ghosting me, hurting those I know to make me suffer. Even left a calling card out of Smiler's entrails. That's how we'll catch the bastard. We don't go to him..."

"We make him come to us." Candace picked up the thread instantly. "But where do we find the monster?"

Johnny's eyes scanned the many maps he'd charted, tracing the Butcher's victims, all vanished and gone. "Knives. Knives and chains. I never thought about it but the pig-faced freak has enough hardware to host his own cooking vid-cast and open a machine-shop all in one. Where is he getting it all?"

Johnny's partner in crime leaned toward the maps, shoulder to shoulder with Johnny, excitement writ across her face. Candace's nail tapped at a large grey blob in the center of the map. "There. Heavy-werks recycling. It's big, centralized, guaranteed to be almost totally automated. I'm willing to bet it's sitting over a hundred different service and waste tunnels. Perfect for a be-aproned serial killer to slip in and out unseen."

Candace grinned at Johnny. This grin left no doubt about the fate of proverbial canary. The bird was done and dinner. "Now we just need to bait the trap."

"Just like Old Burma?"

"Just like Old Burma."

The two shuddered at the memory. Johnny didn't know what highlights his crimson tressed companion was reliving, but J.C. Vid watched a horrid home movie play in his head, one made of jagged memories of wicked knives, harsh yells echoing in the night, and an urban hell painted red with blood and fire. The two aspiring shock-jocks escaped death at the hands of the Glorious Blade, a religious movement that believed redemption could only be achieved through pain and lots of it, by the skin of their teeth and minus some pints of blood between them.

"Let's hope this time works out without a trip to the emergency room."

The red-headed shock-jock flipped Johnny the bird for his reasoned and well thought out protest. "Spoilsport."

Minutes later, with a bit of rapid consulting with Elder Dang, Johnny sat on an impromptu stage with Candace looking right at him, fingers held up and counting down. The mafia don whispered his commands to underlings and sent them running, enraptured at the chance to see a live performance from two favorite vid-stream personalities.

"Alright, Johnny. You're back in the spotlight. Make it good. Smile for the camera."

Johnny leaned toward the eye camera with a lunatic's grin. "Here, piggy, piggy, piggy."

≈

Johnny C. Vid, the man, the myth, the legend, stood in his voluminous trench coat, a puny fleshy creature among hammering industrial machinery, and tried not to run screaming. It was just past midnight in the Heap and evening business was brisk outside. Within the steel cathedral of the Heavywerks recycling foundry, automated systems continued to perform their tasks, tireless smelting down scrap and pounding out sheets of plas-steel to be shaped into any of the thousands of everyday items.

Such as knives, chains, and hooks. All the tools of a dark trade.

So when the Butcher's heavy tread sounded behind him, with a challenging snarl loud enough to be heard over the machines, Johnny wasn't sure whether to be relieved or terrified. The mass of gristle and meat swung 'round the corner, moving cautiously as he glared at the former video-jockey.

The two stood for a moment, their hate forming a bond closer than any lover.

"You know, all the time I was chasing you, I never thought to try and get you to come to me. Even after all the tunnels and the lairs and the twisted remains of your work. Kinda simple, when you think about it. A junkie has needs, after all. You had to get your sick toys from somewhere. Looks like you went right to the source." Johnny waved idly at the industrialized cacophony. "Alright, you bloated piece of shit. Come and get me. Let's end this."

The pig mask regarded its prey, the oversized owner caressing its implements of slaughter.

"Come on! You missed me twice now. Gotta sting, I bet. You even got my invitation. How'd you like that, huh? Sweet little broadcast calling out your Piggly Wiggly ass."

Johnny snorted as he remembered his impromptu broadcast cobbled together with Candace. It played on loop for half a day at as many dives and cheap bars Johnny could manage.

"So, here we are. Been dancing around it long enough. Quit the damn foreplay. Come and get me!" Johnny spread his arms wide, taunting the Butcher. The huge man took two lumbering steps forward before he paused. The Butcher crouched down, more nimble than his bulk and twisted physique should have allowed. One gloved hand reached out and plucked at thin air.

The nearly invisible mono-wire twanged loudly, and gusts of flame roared outward from steam shrouded vents. Had the Butcher tripped the wire, the inferno would have roasted the beast alive.

Lurching past the wire with a greasy chortle, the Butcher stalked toward his prey. Hunger shone through the mask and wicked blades gleamed in the warm glow of the forges. Confusion replaced dark need when said prey stood utterly unconcerned in the face of their impending doom.

"Damn. I figured you'd see the traps but it was worth a shot. Probably wouldn't have gotten me out of debt to them but at least I'd have some leverage to work with."

Johnny felt a thrill of satisfaction as the Butcher's eyes lit up in alarm behind his mask. From gantries, side rooms, and hidden niches in piping, Triad hit squads emerged, guns trained on the trapped beast. Johnny dove to the side as the roar of thunder echoed in the industrial hub, high grade fire arms unloaded into the sadistic monster. Rent and torn by the hail of bullets, the Butcher lunged at Johnny, determined to slay his one escapee. The pig-masked sadist powered through the storm of fire even as chunks of mismatched flesh tore away. With a final lung, the Butcher half fell, half leapt towards the prone vid-jock, a scream of pain and rage escaping his lips.

The killer nearly made it.

The Butcher tumbled to the ground and landed messily in a spreading pool of their own blood, one massive hand still reaching for Johnny's throat and blade clenched in a death grip in the other meaty paw.

Johnny stood up, staring numbly at the fallen beast. *Finally. It's over.*

But even as two black clad clean-up crews body bagged the Butcher's gory remains, Johnny knew it'd only just begun. He and Candace had gone to the Triads, first the Heavenly Gate and then the other families, and shown them the monster of Mr. Vid's nightmares, connecting the thing's sick appetites with the trail of dead in their own ranks.

The Triads did not take kindly to interference in their business.

Candace got some choice info on the Triads, including a promised personal interview with Elder Dang. With some connections from Candace, some financial and muscle backing from the Triads, mixed with Johnny's faded shock-jock skills, they'd baited a trap for the swollen creature.

Even though Johnny had been doing them a favor, he was now deeper in the pockets of the Heavenly Gate crew. Hoa Dang was pleased and not likely to let Johnny go any time soon.

Life was going to be interesting for Mr. Vid in the foreseeable future.

≋

Rosary and Golden Star, two men kept by the Heavenly Gate for their loyalty and muscle if not their intellect, grunted softly with the effort of keeping their uneven and steadily leaking load from tumbling and struggled to haul the Butcher's bloated carcass into the back of an unmarked van.

"S'truth, my dear Golden Star, you'd think this man's sins weigh him down?"

Golden Star, long acclimated to his verbose companion and silent by way of long habit, merely grunted louder as he angled the dead body into the van.

"Aye, that's true. I don't suppose the lad cares if we lay down our Herculean burden. Indifferent child of the earth, he is."

Slamming the doors shut, Golden Star turned to his erstwhile companion with a tired stare.

"Ros, why do you insist on talking like that?"

Rosary smoothed out his midnight colored vestments as he slid into the passenger's side with an aid of offended dignity. "I think it adds some refinement to my position."

Golden Star blinked once, very slowly, as he fired up the vehicle and exhaled noisily though his nose. "We're hired muscle for a criminal organization. There is a bullet riddled body leaking blood in the back of our van. We're freaking goons."

"Then it sounds as if we are the very definition of souls in need of refinement."

As the two continued to bicker, a loud chuff sounded in the back, the stained tarp rising and falling. Beneath it, tortured lungs drew breath and one bloodshot eye tore open.

CHAPTER 1:
A HUMBLE REQUEST

JOHNNY C. VID, the man, the myth, the legend, pulled at the collar of his achingly new suit in a desperate bid to keep it from strangling him. Really, it wasn't the suit's fault. Superbly tailored and immaculately pressed, it poured over Johnny like liquid crimson and gold. It fit like a glove and looked sharp as a razor.

No, the human element was to blame in this scenario.

Not too surprising. A guy tends to get a bit hot under the collar at social affairs with the most powerful crime bosses on the planet.

Triad leaders rubbed elbows in the expansive lobby of the Gentle Fields hotel. Walking sharks in human skin suits, the cold-eyed monsters smiled politely and made friendly chit chat, model guests for their model host, Hoa Dang. He also just so happened to be Johnny's boss.

Boss. Right. Because owner just sounds so crass. Johnny liked to think of himself as an independent contractor but standing at attention, wearing the Heavenly Gates' colors capped with a pin with the three vertical bars of the Heavenly Gates right at the collar, marked him as surely as dogtags with "Fido" written on it. *Guess I'll have to change my working title to "crime boss's bitch."*

"Mr. Vid. You are fidgeting." The quiet reprimand, cast *sotto voce*, slipped between the smiling teeth of Hoa Dang as he oversaw the evening's festivities.

"Apologies, Elder Dang. I'm not used to these high collar scenes...or these high collars."

The Triad don's tone made it clear zero sympathy existed for the shock-jock's plight. "We would expect better behavior from a child, Mr. Vid. Your presence was specifically requested. You should be grateful. Much of this celebration is due to your actions. Take pride in that. And for pity's sake, stop tugging at your collar."

Johnny clamped his hand to his side through force of will. Something he'd had to do a lot recently. Following the fatal shoot-up with the maniacal Butcher, Johnny had been lauded as something of a hero in the criminal underbelly of the Heap. Having been responsible for tracking down and drawing the out the monster that had been carving up their profits, to say nothing of their people, Mr. Vid enjoyed a place of elevated status amongst the great and good of the underworld.

Which meant elevated status for Hoa Dang and the Heavenly Gates Triads as a result.

Johnny's keeper happily paraded the hero of the hour around, having him around like a shiny parrot or trained monkey, making the right sounds to amuse Elder Dang and his peers. There'd been nearly two weeks straight with some sort of celebration every night.

If anyone told me I'd be tired of caviar and champagne when I was burnt-out on Vicarious Reality a few months back, I'd have laughed in their face. The shock-jock glared at the laughing underworld nobles over his drink. *Probably burning more profits in thrown out hors d'oeuvres than the Butcher ever cost them.*

Something nagged the back of Johnny's mind as he watched Elder Dang play host. Intricate and expensive dishes were examined and discarded, tossed straight into the trash as the servers scurried back to the kitchens to do it right. Security was checked again, and again, and once more for good measure. The mafia don was a fury tonight.

A far cry from the gregarious figure Elder Dang usually portrayed.

He's nervous. No, it's more than that. He's scared.

The thought sent a chill down Johnny's spine and his eyes darted around the room. *What could possibly scare Hoa Dang in his own home?*

The answer came moments later, neatly packaged in the form of the gods' gift to mankind entering the lobby. At least, it certainly seemed the figure considered themselves as such. Dark of eye and hair, every inch of the newcomer screamed authority. He didn't simply walk into the room, he took command of it. The man knew he owned the very air they breathed and that they lived only because he allowed it.

Seeing as the late attendee bore the entwined dragon sigil of the Eight-Fold Dynasty, the last part was factually true.

Whispers rippled out in waves through the hotel lobby, the gold and yellow symbol of the Empress sending the great and powerful Triads quaking.

Johnny should have felt the same fear, except shock and disbelief strangled every other emotion into submission. *Sweet Merciful Fates. A Dynast? Here? You'd be just as likely to see a unicorn prancing about the lobby as find an agent of the Empress' Court this close to the Heap.*

The official party line was that the Heap didn't exist, its very existence an embarrassment to the Dynasty and an affront to the Empress' vision for an orderly, clean, and prosperous society. The Empress and her nobles didn't like little things like reality getting in the way of their grand designs. So the Empress' plan advanced smoothly by tacitly ignoring the Heap whenever possible, except to schedule regular dump runs.

A Dynast noble appearing on Kadath, much less in a Triad stronghold at the edge of the Heap wasn't just bad news. It meant something apocalyptic had happened to force the esteemed peerage to stoop so low.

This is what had Hoa Dang so scared.

As the regal guest leisurely made his way through the party, crowd parting like a sea before him, Johnny leaned toward his benefactor.

"Honored Elder, when you said I was requested, did you mean..."

Dang hissed a warning through the pearly gates of his blinding smile. Johnny could put two and two together.

Message received. Shut your face.

The gold and sable clad noble gracefully halted a few feet from Hoa Dang, fractionally inclining his head in greeting. *Cautious. Staying just out of arms reach. Those eyes keep moving.* Johnny guessed this was instinctive, ingrained in the man by years of ruthlessly drilled court etiquette and surviving multiple assassinations.

"Councilman Dang, how good of you to invite us."

The Triad crime boss bowed low at the waist. "The honor is ours, Gentleman Troung. We are humbly grateful that the Eight-Fold graces us."

Another fractional nod. "Indeed. We are pleased you recognize this." Dark eyes turned to regard Johnny, as if peering into his soul. The sweating shock-jock had seen lasers with less focus and intensity. "Let us have tea."

Elder Dang bowed again. "Of course, right this way."

Johnny blinked numbly until one of the genuflecting staff nudged him along behind the Triad boss. The trio vanished into a side room, surrounded by bowing staff and burly guards, leaving a wake of confused murmurs and whispered speculation behind them. The rumor mill would be busy that evening, with wild guesses feeding on one another. One thing all agreed upon: Elder Dang always threw the best parties.

≈

Johnny sat rigidly at attention between the Dynastic noble and the Triad crime boss, trying to both take his cues from Elder Dang and still gape at the impossible sight before him. The incredibly mundane impossible sight before him. Once past the shock, Johnny marveled at how physically unimposing the Dynast was. Sitting at ease, Gentleman Troung looked like a well-preserved man in his middle years. Of course, having access to the Dynasty's advanced medical treatments that put him anywhere between thirty and a hundred and thirty. He wasn't even done up in the beautifying enhancement work every respectable shock-jock and public speaker underwent.

Regardless, Gentleman Troung radiated a palpable energy, a quiet authority that stemmed from someone utterly at peace with their place in the universe.

Right at the top of the shit heap.

After a small eternity of polite drivel and empty-nothing speak over tea and sweet treats, the Dynastic envoy set their cup down with a small but audible click. "We appreciate your offer of tea. It is heartening to see traces of civilization, so far from Court."

Elder Dang took the backhanded compliment with a small bow and a smile.

The Gentleman turned to regard Johnny again with the same penetrating gaze as before. "We have come here on a matter of some importance. Our agents reported an event of some interest. An alliance of Triad families, gathered together to hunt a shadowy killer in their midst. A wretched beast, by all accounts. At the heart of it all, one disgraced news personality who survived the monster's affections not once but three times, living when all others perished. Most impressive."

"I prefer 'freelance operative' these days, honored Gentleman."

A wintery smile touched the noble's face at the audacity and Hoa Dang looked ready to puke. "We need a man of your skills, including your luck. Especially your luck, one might say." Porcelain cup raised to lips for a delicate sip. "One of our good servants has gone missing. While it galls us to admit it, they have been abducted by parties unknown. We request your aid to find them."

Johnny licked his lips and tried a bit more impudence. "I say this without presumption, but, don't you have a host of more qualified agents of your own?"

"Indeed we do. But what matters is where they vanished. They vanished while investigating the Heap. More specifically the Basement."

"The Basement? As in UNDER the Boneyard? It's a lost city, nothing there but the dead, the dying, and the deranged. What in the name of the Pure Lands made them go there?"

Blizzards held more warmth than the Gentleman's eyes. "Our orders, Mr. Vid. Therein lies the crux of our dilemma. We cannot be seen investigating the area. As you know, it is official Court policy that such a blemish on Her Realm does not exist. To admit losing an agent would be bad enough, but to admit sending another to investigate it...we cannot permit this loss of face. Thus, such a mission calls for an individual with a cunning mind, a stubborn will, and a penchant for surviving where all others failed." The shark tooth grin left no doubt whom Gentleman Troung was referring to.

Johnny could still put two and two together. He didn't like the way the math added up.

The squirming shock-jock looked at Hoa Dang, only to be greeted with a piercing stare. No words were said. None were needed. Refuse and die. *Two plus two.*

Johnny smiled weakly and bowed his head. "I humbly accept this honor, Gentleman Troung."

≈

The thing about detective work is that it takes a lot of effort, a lot of time, and a whole lot of boredom. Johnny threaded along the cracked pavement, chomping on the last bit of his pretzel banh-mi as he checked his messages for any new leads. *Nothing. Nada. Zilch.*

Slumping into a park bench with a sigh, Johnny rubbed his face. He'd trudged from one end of the Heap to the other, asking all the right questions to all the wrong people. Johnny had even leaned on his status and celebrity as a Triad goon. It was a surreal experience for the former VR junkie. *The same street toughs that would have beat my ass for looking at them funny are now bowing and scraping for the big bad Triad. Yeah, that's me; Johnny C. Vid, Triad spook extraordinaire.*

Still, even after asking nicely, not even a blip. All he'd gotten were more of Pang's ghost stories. The street folk kept saying the same thing; angry ghosts wandered the wasteland-city, snatching up people without a trace. People just up and disappeared. It sounded ominously familiar. Johnny reminded himself, not for the first time that day, that the Butcher was dead. Now only normal people wanted to kill him.

It proved cold comfort for the current job.

As he'd left, Gentleman Troung casually mentioned that the agent in question was an Assessor; a direct representative of the Dynasty and the Empress. "A Tax Man? I'm looking for a Tax Man?" His outburst had not been appreciated nor his debased slang term for one the Dynasty's finest espionage agents.

The former shock-jock's hopes of making it out alive dropped further. If one of the genetically and cybernetically enhanced wet-work machines of the Dynasty got themselves nixed, Johnny's odds at survival looked pretty grim.

One might be forgiven for accusing the dragooned detective of dragging his feet. Which, judging by the pointed reminders from his twin keepers, Johnny's keepers certainly were. Closing out the second week of Johnny's fruitless investigation, a call on his wrist-comm revealed the glaring face of Elder Dang and the falsely serene face of Gentleman Troung sitting nearby.

Uh oh.

"Gentleman! Elder! How good to see you both."

Dang cut right through the pleasantries, an utterly disastrous sign as far as Johnny was concerned. "We expect an update, Mr. Vid. We expect that you have found something of use, of merit. We expect results."

"Look, my esteemed peers, these things take time."

Elder Dang looked ready to explode, but held his tongue as the Gentleman took a leisurely sip of tea. "We understand such things, which is why we have been so generous. We expected results, however, in a matter of days."

"Days? Days!? This is the Heap. Millions, probably billions of lives crammed into sprawling concrete, slum habs, and plas-steel towers. That's not even taking the freaking tunnels into account. Warrens of lost people, places you only find if you know about it or go excavating for buried freaking treasure. It's not just about length but depth, too. Three dimensional fuckery at its finest. And you, good Gentleman, want to find one person, in the Basement. Miles of a buried, forgotten city stretching gods only know how far down, home to gods only know what, in a place so dangerous it doesn't even exist on official maps."

Only winding down from his rant did Johnny C. Vid, the man, the myth, the legend, realize he'd mouthed off to an aristocrat of the Eight-Fold Dynasty, a being who could and would end him, painfully and messily, without a glimmer of hesitation or remorse.

As such, the very foolish man held his breath and prayed very hard to every god he knew as Gentleman Troung languidly drank his tea. "Very well. We have heard your appeal. You have three days. If you cannot procure our agent in that time, you will disappear as well."

The communication screen went dark and Johnny counted his blessings in between rapid rounds of cursing.

CHAPTER 8:
A MEETING OF THE MINDS

They say desperation is the mother of invention, but after the conference call with the Elder Dang and Gentleman Troung and their ultimatum, Johnny C. Vid didn't feel mighty inventive. He just felt desperate.

Why else would I be creeping through the Boneyard?

A morbid sense of déjà vu crept over Johnny as he picked his way through the towering piles of scrap and junk as cautiously as he could. *The last time I came here, I ended up dangling on a hook in the den of a pig-faced madman.* This time it wasn't addiction that drove the shock-jock onward, but a different kind of desperation. *I'd rather not be disappeared like those ghost-victims Pang mentioned.*

Johnny knew that Gentleman Troung did not make idle threats.

Even among the destitution of the Heap, the Boneyard and its Basement held a special reputation. A cancerous pit of forgotten dreams, a monument to the callousness of the powerful, the piles of junk erased a buried city beneath its rotted mass and swallowed up any lost souls foolish enough to come by. Only the most deranged or desperate came there willingly. *And I know which camp I fall under.*

The shock-jock tromped through the piles of filth as carefully as he could, every nerve on edge. A distant clang sent Johnny scrambling for cover, taking refuge in what might have been the front half of a bus. Many panicked heartbeats later, the shock-jock peeked out from behind the broken shell and moved forward. The drama repeated itself several times, every sound sending Johnny diving into any nearby hiding spot. As Johnny calmed his pounding heart, he looked at his wrist-comm and winced at the time.

This could take a while.

Hours passed as he wandered through the labyrinth mess. When the dim light of the setting sun made shadowed valleys between the mountains of castoffs, Johnny sighed in frustration. *Can't stay here after night fall and I can't leave empty handed. Shit, I hate this stinking hole!*

Johnny kicked a grimy piece of a busted children's toy and sent the neon plastic and rubber lump flying through the air. It rebounded off a huge block of metal with a hollow clank. Instantly Johnny's ears perked with interest. *Clank? That's an engine block the size of Aunt Jenny. It'd take battering ram to ring that thing like a bell.*

Johnny tiptoed to the curious slab and gave it a hearty smack. Rather than stand firm, like a giant hunk of metal ought to, the whole thing slid a bit. Further experimentation escalated from rapping, to kicking, to poking the block with a broken mop handle. *This thing is as empty as my bank account. Why is it out here?* His old investigative reporter instincts flickering on after years of disuse, Johnny bent down and looked at the dirt around the curious metal mystery. Brushing aside a thin layer of dirt revealed that the whole thing rested on a track. Johnny ignored the lengthening shadows and eagerly shoved his weight into the block, nearly toppling over as the hollow metal frame rolled aside with ease. *Alright, turns out it rests on well-oiled hidden tracks.* A realization that only brought Johnny trepidation. Well-oiled meant well used. Tiny lights illuminated a tunnel delving into the mountain of junk.

Might as well see how far the rabbit hole goes. Ducking to avoid smacking his head in the confined space, Johnny C. Vid dove into the unknown.

Turned out the unknown only lasted for a short jaunt. Fumbling through a city's block of awkward crouch-walking, Johnny popped out into a large metal chamber. Faint lumen strips lit the area enough to see while still leaving a patina of shadows to cloud distant details. A familiar smell hit Johnny's nostrils, unwashed clothes and long ignored messes faded to stains. Something else lay behind the stink but he couldn't put a name to it. All around him blanket rolls and other signs of habitation dotted the dimly lit room. An eerie sensation of deja vu washed over Johnny, raising up paranoid terrors in the back of his mind.

He'd lived in the street camps, under bridges and in derelict factories, wherever you could get an ounce of cover from the elements. Johnny knew those camps too damn well and this wasn't them.

The rolls made orderly rows, arranged in equal, regimented spaces. No discarded cig-packs or empty bottles dotted the area. There weren't even newspapers or porno-slates laying around. None of the normal distractions and simple pleasures such displaced souls availed themselves too.

The whole thing felt more like a military camp than a homeless den to the street savvy Johnny.

This isn't right. Doesn't smell right either.

A few steps into the room, smoke tickled his nostrils, the rich smell of incense rather instead of cigarettes. What should have smelt like a dumpster filled alley smelled more like a temple. Under that out of place aroma, the same familiar smell persisted. Something coppery and sharp tugged at Johnny's hindbrain but he couldn't place it. He followed the anachronistic scent, so out of place amongst the grime and oil, past the sleeping bags and through hastily erected hodgepodge dividers of tarp and sheet metal.

As he followed his nose, the shock-jock dodged around soiled cloth and rusting metal, a nagging sense of familiarity beating at him. He'd always had a knack for remembering things, picking out those little details that let him follow up on hunches, and Johnny remember places well.

Pretty sure I'd remember a Temple de Street Bum.

The sense of wrongness continued alongside the unnerving impression of a place of worship. Whoever dwelt here were true believers. In what exactly, Johnny wasn't sure.

Rather than the usual profanities and garbled half-formed sentences associated with life on the streets, the scrawled graffiti was just as incomprehensible but infinitely more bizarre. Time and again, odd missives decorated the partitions and walls, blaring cryptic messages such as "The Unworthy have Chained the Angels" and others declaring the end was nigh in nihilistic scrawls. The theological and apocalyptic merged and through them all a common motif emerged. Endlessly the dwellers, whom Johnny had begun to think of as a cult, venerated something called "the Black Queen."

The nameless devotees pledged their undying devotion to the Black Queen, attributed otherworldly powers to it, and paradoxically claimed her to be both near and far, lost and indelibly bound within the mind and soul of whoever wrote the crazed prayers. Between these liturgies, a sinuous infinity symbol, two snakes intertwined beneath a crown, repeated itself again and again.

This Queen of theirs must be some hot shit.

Johnny prowled onward silently, trying to make sense of the disturbing iconography.

Everything fell away when Johnny saw the mask.

Cradled on a red-stained plinth framed by candelabra, lay a pig mask. The Pig Mask. Its rough stitches cut jagged paths of hate on its surface and the empty eye holes glared balefully at the shock-jock.

Realization hit Johnny like a fist in the gut. *Nononohe'sdeadpleaseno.*

His mind reeled as he frantically looked around. He mentally cut through the adornments and trashy walling looking at the dark cavern in its moldering entirety. He saw the Butcher's torture slabs covered in silk curtains, adorned with sweet offerings and wilting flowers. Glancing up, Johnny noticed the chains remained but were now bedecked with bits of bone tied through their loops and skulls dangling from their hooks.

It had been cleaned up, re-purposed, divided into separate chambers, and decorated like a temple to a god of slaughter but the hateful mask brought everything into sickening clarity. Johnny stood in the den of the Butcher, where the shock-jock had hung alongside other damned souls like slabs of beef in a larder.

Stumbling against a hanging sheet, Johnny tore it in two. Behind it, crimson remains lay piled high, stuffed into bloody sacks. Other masks, graven and mocking imagery of animals, looked down from their perches on racks, robes fanning beneath them. Po's rumors took on a horrible new scope.

Whoever they were, this religious cult knew who the Butcher was. They knew and revered his twisted works. Imitation, as they say, was the sincerest form of flattery.

Johnny ran. He ran as fast as he could. He stumbled, fell, slammed into tunnel walls and tripped over relics of a dead city but he never stopped his desperate flight out of the pit.

≈

"The Butcher's alive."

Without preamble or warning, Johnny C. Vid pushed into Hoa Dang's study. The Triad crime boss didn't look up from his data-slate only giving an exasperated sigh in acknowledgment. Fortunately, Hoa Dang also waved off the lurking Triad guard who reached for her gun to ventilate Johnny for his bad manners. "Hello, Mr. Vid."

"The Butcher's alive. I don't know how, I don't know where..." Johnny diatribe stopped as he studied the Triad boss's face. Johnny had chased enough ambulances to know shock and disbelief. That wasn't it. He'd also played enough poker to see through a bluff.

"You knew."

Quick as a viper, Hoa Dang gripped the shock-jock's arm in an iron vice and dragged him close. "Do not speak of such things so loudly. You endanger us all." He let Johnny go and dismissed the guards as Johnny rubbed feeling back into his arm.

"How long have you known?"

Dang let out a heavy sigh. "Since the night we first killed the beast. My clean-up crew did their duty as they always have. Packed up the body into their van and drove off to dispose of its befouled remains. They never checked into the morgue. We found the van dumped in a ditch, the remains of my men inside." Any trace of a kindly uncle vanished in a flush of angry red. "Rosary and Golden Star are dead. Butchered. Their body parts stacked like fire-wood. The creature was nowhere to be found."

"Why didn't you tell me?" Johnny closed in, face to face with Elder Dang, seething with anger.

"Mr. Vid!" The steely retort pierced Johnny's outrage, who suddenly realized he was staring down one of the most dangerous men in the Heap. "We did not want to alarm you then and we do not want to alarm you now. Our best killers are hunting that creature down. No one escapes the Triads. You would do well to remember that." Gone was all trace of the kindly uncle, replaced with a stone faced and steely eyed killer. This was the Hoa Dang who ran one the largest criminal syndicates on Kadath and would not take lip from an upstart underling. Johnny might have had a well of good faith but Hoa Dang's stare made it clear he tread on very thin ice. "Now, we need you to remain calm, keep silent, and do your duty. Any word of this will cause us to lose face, make us appear weak, and we cannot afford that in front of the other Triad families and certainly not in front of the Dynasty. If that should happen, you needn't worry about the Butcher ending you. Gentleman Troung and I will make certain of that."

Johnny glared, but remained silent.

"Now, do you have any news? Any idea where the Assessor may be?"

The shock-jock sighed heavily. "Yeah, I think I just might. I found...something. I'm not sure what. But it looks like we're dealing with more than just one maniac now."

Johnny described his stumbling in the Boneyard and his discovery of the Butcher's reclaimed lair. "Someone had set up shop there, Hoa Dang. Lots of someones. They've been carrying on the Butcher's work. Hell, the sick bastards seem to revere him or something. That and something called the Black Queen, whatever the hells that is."

Elder Dang's face darkened like a thundercloud. "This does not bode well."

"I agree, honored Elder. Whoever they are, they're organized, numerous, and probably responsible for the more deaths than your hit squads." Dang's face indicated he did care for the shock-jock's flippant comparison. Johnny hurried on. "I'm not sure, but these mask wearing ghosts seem to be the only candidates are fit the bill as being able to disappear an Assessor without the Triads knowing."

"Very well, Mr. Vid. How do you plan to remedy this?"

Johnny cocked his head. "Mind if I borrow a flashlight?"

≈

Johnny had gone beyond desperate, right past divine bargaining, and straight into blind panic. I *thought I only had to worry about normal crazies trying to kill me. Now I've got the Butcher, who is both not dead and has a freaking fan club by the look of things. How can things get any worse?*

Of course, the dragooned detective kept this mental diatribe going to distract himself from the fact that he was walking into a tenebrous hell of twisting tunnels so far off the grid it made Johnny's tenement look like the Gentle Fields Hotel.

Dressed in black, like he'd seen in countless spy vids, Johnny carried a mountaineering backpack with assorted food, water, and tools. The beam of his flashlight pierced the oppressive darkness, a thin spear of dawn showing his path. Down and down Johnny went, following his gut and best guesses. The walls were a mix of packed dirt and forgotten bits of civilization, light catching on pieces from crushed cars, cracked pipes, bent girders, and soda pop cans. All the detritus of the people once living here.

The carved sconces with burning tallow candles next to hollow-eyed skulls, marked new tenants. Snapping off his light and letting his eyes adjust to dim glow, Johnny marveled at the meticulousness of the set up. A ritual orderliness hung about the placement of each victim, an almost reverent adornment of the flayed remains.

The Butcher's lairs were monstrous but this is just creepy.

Following the macabre breadcrumbs, Johnny crept forward, sneaking as best he could dressed in all black surrounded by colors more at home in a bakery than hidden tunnels beneath a dead city. *It seemed like a good idea at the time. Who expects psycho cultists to decorate in warm tones and soft ambient lighting? I just hope I don't end up like their other dinner guests.*

After creeping along for what seemed like hours, the tunnel dumped Johnny into a large open chamber, a confluence of tunnel mouths dotting the cavern at uneven intervals, crude earthen ramps reaching each rough wound in the earth. At the heart of the cavern, festooned with votive offerings like an altar, stood a humming machine. Johnny clicked his teeth down to trap an appreciative whistle from echoing in the spacious room.

That certainly isn't local to the Heap. Cutting edge, whatever it is. I wonder if even Gentleman Troung's seen anything like it. Johnny examined the blinking black box, circling round it. *Military. Gotta be. It almost looks like part of a Thinking Ship.*

His eyes, then his hands, followed the technological artifact's sleek curves, caressing it like a work of art. The Thinking Ships of the Dynasty enabled the Empress to keep her iron grip on the Eight-Fold System. Powerful warships guided by self-aware, independent Artificial Intelligences, they had almost single handedly pushed the Terran fleet out of the system during the Liberation Wars. Thinking machines, bound by honor and loyalty to the greater good, they battled alongside their mortal crews with a terrible ferocity and skill. The Thinking Ships served not because they were compelled to, but because they it was the noble thing to do. Each one was as much a hero of the Dynasty as their flesh and blood counterparts and their inner workings were a closely guarded state secret. Far beyond anything a bunch of knife wielding loonies could cobble together.

Here I am, touching part of the Dynasty's most prized war vessels. Candace would kill for a scoop like this. Heh, she'd probably kill me for it, first. The smooth composite shell gave way to a nest of wiring, nestled around a ridged, rubbery mass. The shock-vid recoiled as he realized he was basically fondling a human brain.

Of course, it wasn't a bit of grey matter simply ripped from its fleshy carriage. This was a Lifeline; a home away from home for a human brain. Reinforced with latex, rubber, and several advanced devices, including a filtration lung, the brain lived in a cybernetic panic bubble of its own, surviving completely independent of a body. It was a trauma ward, a safety jar, and a life preserver all in one. Only high explosives would have bothered the brain box. Even should the body be completely destroyed, the person's brain lived on, ready for transplant into a new body. It was an expensive and highly technical procedure, one reserved for only the richest, or most important, of persons.

It also happened to be hooked directly into a blinking device that shouldn't exist in the Heap.

"Mr. Tax Man, I presume?"

Gingerly, Johnny removed the cables and hefted the brain box. *Certainly looks like my guy. At least what's left of them. Only one way to make sure.* Looking around, he snaked a cable from his cyberport and linked himself directly to the brain.

The screaming hit Johnny like jagged glass between his eyes. Not screams of agony but screams of rage. The unbroken litany of death threats was impressive for its width, breath, and inventiveness.

"Calm down, I'm here to help!" With such a cacophonous tirade going off in his head, Johnny instinctively shouted at the galvanized brain.

Who are you? Identify yourself! The voice in Johnny's head was sharp, refined, and unquestionably authoritative.

"I'm Johnny C. Vid. Here to get you out." Decidedly feminine impressions ghosted through the mind link, faded body imprints of the now absent physical form. "Wait, I thought you were Tax Men?"

Indignation washed over the shock-jock so hard he wanted to slap himself. *We are ASSESSORS, you uncultured swine. We observe, measure, and when neces-*

sary, correct matters to fit the Empress' superior vision for the galaxy. Simply because your uncouth, ignorant, idiotic barbarization of our tongue misses the point is no fault of ours. Johnny recoiled in his own head. Captured, lobotomized, and tortured in her own mind and Johnny got the sense she was more offended by his use of slang than the depredations of her captors.

"Damn, sorry! For a brain in a jar, you're very rude to your rescuer."

I am not a brain in a jar! I am Nhi Troung, servant of the Empress, may She rule forever, and Assessor of the first class. Why are you even speaking aloud? Our minds are in conjunction. Do you want us to get caught?

"Well, I'm not used to having some crazy lady yelling in my mind, so this helps normalize things. It isn't every day we are deep in the bowels of a murder cult den where no one can find...our...bones." Johnny's eyes snapped up and darted around the cavern. "Shit."

Indeed. Did you not think of the consequences of an incautious tongue in the middle of a "murder cult den?"

"I did just now." Johnny hissed. "Besides, a cautious tongue didn't seem to save you from getting a free lobotomy."

You insolent cur!

Their back and forth was cut short by a bird masked cultist in black and white robes walking into the chamber, whistling as she polished a bare skull. She looked up. Their eyes made contact. Time froze.

"Hi?" Johnny opened hopefully.

Instantly the robed figured turned and ran back into the tunnel, screaming at the top of their lungs. "Apostate! The Apostate is here! It is he, the Lamb with Teeth!"

Confused as hell but taking the hint, Johnny ran for his life.

Flying through the tunnels, the black clad rescuer tucked his grey matter package under his arm like a rugby player running down the field.

Turn right, now!

Johnny nearly jumped into the tunnel ceiling. "I'd forgotten you were still plugged in."

It is a good thing I am. I will help you find your way back to the surface.

Johnny panted as he followed the Assessor's directions, guided through tunnel after winding tunnel. "You remember the way?"

Of course. Eidetic memory. However, I am using your memories to fill any gaps in my knowledge. You have a strong mind, one that endures well. It is worn but sturdy.

"Thank you?" Johnny felt torn between violation and pride.

You are welcome. The Assessor sounded utterly sincere in her response.

Johnny muttered something unkind at his brain-bound traveling companion and didn't notice the robed figure in his path until the two collided with a bone jarring thud. Sprawled on the floor, the cultist clutched his gut while Johnny clutched the brain case. If anything happened to it, Gentleman Troung would have him beaten, flogged, and charred. Then he'd get real nasty.

Get up! Block high! Strike now!

Johnny reacted to the mind-speak without question, hands and arms moving, though with more alacrity than precision. He felt his limbs swing almost of their accord.

Scuffling and wrestling in the dirt, the cultist dove for the knife shaken loose in their collision. Coming up into a crouch, they found Johnny's foot already in motion, landing squarely between the knife wielder's braced legs.

Ding. Direct hit. With a high-pitched squawk the masked cultist dropped to the dirt, clutching ruined family jewels.

Unscrupulous. Unorthodox. Dirty. I didn't even have to prompt you. Nhi's sending carried the pride of a teacher watching a pupil excel.

Pulsing back feelings of gratitude, Johnny snatched up the knife, shoved it into his pack, and hightailed it down the tunnel.

A good thing, since from the sound of thundering boots, a whole host of friends were coming behind him. Pushing past a ludicrously corroded door, Johnny slammed it behind him with a shriek of tortured hinges and slumped against the barrier.

"I haven't been this popular since my shock-jock days."

Indeed. Your debauched escapades with your adoring fans are quite...memorable.

Johnny went rigid. "How did you...oh, Merciful Fates, you're rooting around in my memories, aren't you?"

I am inquisitive by nature and training, Mr. Vid. Though I object to your terms. "Rooting around" would be vulgar and crass. I am simply reviewing immediately presentable data.

"Terrific!" Johnny shouted at the top of his lungs, purely out of spite. "Help me review the immediately presentable room to see if we can live long enough to get back home."

Two pairs of eyes scanned the room, Nhi's disembodied sight invisibly tracking with Johnny's. They seemed to be trapped in some sort of storage area that doubled as a guard station or break room. Cleaning supplies sat on top of boxes of lightbulbs and other common household items. Dishes sat drying on a rack next to a sink. Another closed door stood opposite the one they entered, equally dilapidated. A rickety table and destitute chairs stood in the center, no use to the one-bodied duo. A child could have pushed past the flimsy seating arrangement. It would do little to halt a horde of blood-thirsty lunatics. Only when their eyes rested upon the bags of industrial grade fertilizer, gallons of styling gel, and chest high aero-methane torch canisters that possibilities emerged.

"Hey, this might sound crazy but have you seen..."

Screaming Jiangshi 6: Terror of the Tongs? Of course! We have everything here to give our pursuers as nasty a surprise as Chan did his ghoulish foes.

"I've always wanted to recreate that scene." Johnny sighed happily, hurriedly gathering up the supplies.

Me too. Pyromaniacal glee oozed into the Assessor's composed cadence.

Once Johnny had the brain safely stowed in his backpack, wires trailing to his port like a twisted umbilical cord, they got to work. After Johnny sloppily jammed a pile of gel, fertilizer, and methane tanks in the middle of the room, the shock-jock oozed a trail of jelly to a small barricade cobbled together from the remaining bags of dung and flimsy table. Even as the door gave way, Johnny lit the highly flammable hair product. The frenzied cultists gaped in horror and rapidly backpedaled as fire raced along the gooey fuse.

The resulting explosion would have made the most jaded action-fan proud.

Ears ringing with the explosion and choking on the acrid smoke, Johnny half ran, half stumbled past the moaning cultists, staggering through the tunnels to burst into the sunlight above. He tore through mile long ruins, darting between mountains of junk without pause, ignoring the voice in his head trying to be heard over the ringing in his ears. The former shock-jock finally tumbled through the gates of the nearest Triad owned pawn shop with a jangle of tiny bells, where he promptly fell to his knees and threw up.

"I. Need. To. Speak. To. Elder. Dang." The request, interrupted by large gasps of air and punctuated by the ripe smell of bile carried desperation on each word.

The attendants behind the desk looked at one another, looked at Johnny, then silently pointed to the comm-unit on his wrist. Johnny looked down in shock as his mental piggy-backer laughed uproariously in his head. You didn't have to be a mind reader to recognize "I told you so."

≈

Patched up with enough painkillers to tranquilize a horse, Johnny almost felt human again. *I'll say this for the Triads; they give you the good shit.*

After a harried call reached Elder Dang, the Heavenly Gate Triads reacted with astonishing speed. A fleet of black vehicles swarmed the pawn shop, red and gold foot soldiers spilling out like bees from an overturned hive. In no time flat, the gangsters had Johnny and his incumbent brain ride-along secured and pumped full of lovely pain-numbing drugs.

Nhi gave a mental grunt of disapproval as Johnny sighed. *I question the wisdom of giving you narcotics.*

Johnny gave a sour grunt back. "Because I'm an ex-junkie?"

Yes.

"My vice was Vicarious Reality, oh noble Assessor. Totally different joy buzzer."

Charming.

The Triad goons did their best not to look concerned at their precious guest having an argument with himself. Something about the big bad Triad kneebreakers quaking in their boots around little old Johnny C. Vid sent the shock-jock into titters. Maybe it was the drugs.

"Don't fret, ladies and gentlemen. It's all in my head."

"We care more about *who* is in your head, Mr. Vid."

Johnny looked up to find Gentleman Troung striding through the crowd of crimson suits as utterly unconcerned by their heavily armed presence as he would a host of school children. Hoa Dang followed in his wake like a concerned younger brother.

Ah, Uncle. It is good to see you again.

"Uncle?" That cut through Johnny's buzz.

The Dynastic noble smiled briefly and nodded. "Good. My Assessor is with you. We would speak with her now." It was not a request.

Johnny unsnapped the brain-in-a-backpack and handed the mess over to the noble. A hiss-click and haptic feedbacks in the Dynast's hands linked with the Nhi-box, much sleeker than Johnny's cord dangling mess. Johnny wondered just how much of Gentleman Troung was flesh and how much was metal.

Questions for later. Now, I gotta tell the bosses. Here's hoping they don't kill the messenger.

"Elder Dang, we need to talk about the Butcher. No bones about it, he's got a fan club. A very active and organized one. They were the ones that snagged the Assessor."

Both the crime boss and the Dynast's face grew grave as the shock-jock recounted his tale, augmented by input from niece-in-a-jar if Gentleman Troung's nods were any indication.

"This, um, cult. I didn't catch their name, so that's what I'm calling them. There is no way they should have been able to find, much less take down the Assessor. From what little I know of her, of any Assessor, she should have eaten them for breakfast."

Crow's feet crinkled the corners of Gentleman Troung's eyes "We doubt they would have been much to her taste."

Johnny plowed on, his story poured out in an adrenaline and drug fueled slurry. "Then there's the tech. What I saw down there shouldn't exist in the Heap, or anywhere else outside of black-ops laboratories and Thinking Ships. I doubt even a Dynast noble like you would have something that bleeding edge. There's more, though. These crazies worshipped the Butcher. They took his mask. His mask. You understand? The monster loves it like his face. If they have that stitched pig-face, they have that monster tucked away somewhere. Maybe he's working for them. Maybe they work for him. Maybe they're one big happy murder family, I don't know. What I do know, is that this isn't some isolated group of crazies. This is a conspiracy. A powerful one. With what I saw down there, I think it reaches all the way to Her Sublime Majesty's Court."

The nearby Triads held their breath, even Elder Dang. The official line was that the Eight-Fold Dynasty did not and could not make mistakes. To suggest otherwise, particularly in earshot of a Dynast noble, meant an immediate and messy end for the speaker and possibly anyone in a three-block radius, just to make sure.

Instead of an imminent demise, Mr. Vid's sacrilegious proclamation earned a smile from the Gentleman. "We knew you had potential. You have once again rewarded our faith in you."

"I'm glad. Because I'm going after them. After him."

The arched eyebrow asked several questions.

"That bastard's mine. I'm finishing this. Permanently. To do that, I need some things from you."

If Elder Dang had paled at Johnny's slander against the Dynasty, he went corpse white at the audacity of Johnny's demanding anything of Gentleman Troung. The Dynast cocked his head, engaged in a private conference with his niece. After several very tense minutes, the Gentleman's eyes refocused on Johnny.

"You have a plan. Our goals coincide. The Empress smiles upon this. Tell us what you need."

Chapter 9:
Reunion

JOHNNY STALKED through the darkened nightmare scape of the Boneyard with determined vigor. A whisper-suit muted his every step, swallowed his ambient noise. Vampyre night-visors aided his sight, a tiny map and helpful arrow glowing in his sight guided him through the green tinted mountains of urban wreckage.

He moved like a ghost through the graveyard city. It should have comforted him. In truth, Johnny felt the hairs on the back of his head stand up. Everything was too quiet. In the Heap, there was always noise. Darkest night didn't kill the pulse of the megapolis, only changed it. Mobiles rumbled by, street lights and lumens hummed, and always, always, always there was the sound of people. Quarreling, laughing, and screwing each other. Literally and figuratively. Day or night, people never stopped in the Heap, the moving blood cells in that great body of concrete and steel.

Small wonder then, that the stillness of the Boneyard unnerved the shock-jock.

Last time it was this quiet, I got impaled by a pig-faced freak with a necro-fetish.

Seemed a bit of a sick joke that Johnny worked to find that same monster again. *This time's different. This time, I'm ending you, you sick bastard.* Johnny touched his dataport gingerly, thinking of the trump card stored within his cybernetics, a silver bullet to take out the sadistic murderer should conventional ordinance fail.

Johnny passed unseen and unheard through the miles of castoffs. Nothing impeded his way. No signs of movement or sentries anywhere. Johnny paused at the mouth of a tunnel into Basement. Not the way he'd entered before, this was a smaller exit, a secret back way used by Assessor Nhi Troung to access the heart of the maze-like warren of tunnels.

Johnny sucked in a breath, stifled the urge to scream, and ducked into the claustrophobic space.

As he moved through tunnel after tunnel, Johnny came across signs of hasty abandonment. The sick votive candles still burned, but dents, scratches, and scrapes along the wall and floors showed incautious lugging of materials. Footprints created a kaleido-scope carpet on the bare dirt.

Must not have liked us kicking over their little anthill. I only hope the Butcher is still here.

By the time Johnny reached the broader living quarters, night-visors abandoned in the gently lit burrows, he could tell something wasn't right. Mr. Vid squinted in the dim light but his nose told him what was wrong before his eyes adjusted. *Ozone, oil, bleach, and copper. One surefire recipe for murder and clean up jobs.* The former shock-jock knew the smell of a sloppily cleaned crime scene from his journal-ism days. Living with the Triads strengthened that familiarity. As his eyes scanned the darkness, the full scope of the carnage unfolded.

Bullet holes dotted the walls, barricades cobbled together out of furniture and loose junk, then shat-tered in a struggle. Blotchy pale spots showed signs of cleaning chemicals as though someone tried to scrub out copious blood stains. The drag marks at the entrance suddenly seemed more ominous.

The cultists weren't running from us. They were run-ning from something down here. Something big. Something ruthless. Something with a taste for blood.

Johnny dredged up his long dormant journal-ist skills and turned a clinical eye on the scene. All gunfire seemed to follow one moving target, shift-ing from spot to spot. Clusters of bullet holes, pale splashes of bleach, and broken furniture marked the struggle, clear as a chalk outline on a sidewalk. They had been shooting at something that ripped through them without stopping, leaving a trail of victims in its wake.

But no bodies. A corpse-less slaughter. Someone had taken the bodies. No doubt remained for Johnny. The Butcher's handiwork, as surely as if the monster had signed his name.

The cultists cleaned up and ran. That means they either subdued him and lugged him somewhere more secure, drove the psycho off, or the beast is off somewhere indulging his sick little hobby. Maybe they killed the pig-faced bastard. Maybe. And maybe the Empress Herself will appear and give me a gold medal and my own starcraft.

Johnny plunged deeper into the facility, following the panorama of carnage, the smell of fresh blood, and a deepening thrum of active machinery.

The packed trash and earth tunnels gave way to polished steel corridors and buzzing fluorescent lumens, bare metal and harsh antiseptic lighting. Most of the lights were smashed, rather recently judging by the sparks and shattered plas-steel on the floor, but the place reeked of the same military orderliness of the shrine Johnny had stumbled upon in the ruins of the Butcher's lair.

The corridors were painted in the same mind-numbing functional military trifecta of olive, brown, and gunmetal grey. Evenly spaced doors, heavy duty and reinforced, were marked in simple spray-stenciled numerals. Only the blood and bullet holes gave it an atmosphere better suited a mad scientist's lair. Beakers and vials of all kind lay strewn about, most shattered, some not. Snake-like wires still ran to sockets, large industrial cords hardwired into the superstructure. Bits of technology, the same sleek black tech that Johnny found Nhi's brain locked into, lay scattered about. Broken or simply pieces abandoned in a hurry, Johnny couldn't tell. One large door lay crumpled and battered, unable to contain the malicious force inside.

The Butcher had claimed the cultist's sanctum, the worshipped turning on the worshippers.

He's still here. I can feel it.

With a surreal sense of certainty, of destiny, Johnny C. Vid, the man, the myth, the legend, walked into the beast's lair. A strange instinct guided each step. Even without it, finding the Butcher was simple enough for anyone with eyes. The killer left broken bodies and blood spots as unholy breadcrumbs behind him. No cleanup this far into the cultists' former hidey hole. This was the Butcher's domain, uncontested.

Johnny walked past a gaping opening, its reinforced and padded door lying broken on the floor, painted crimson with whoever had the misfortune of standing in the Butcher's way. The former shock-jock heard the snuffling and smelt his pig-faced adversary long before he saw him, the charnel cocktail of oil, death, and musky steroid-chems. When Johnny finally found the Butcher, he was playing with a victim.

One of the cultists was crucified on a jagged framework of metal made of bent medical gurneys. Leather straps held the ruined body together in cruel parodies of bandages. One particularly thick strap wrapped around the cultist's throat, constricting his air way as gravity did its work. The masked zealot slowly hung himself as his severed muscles failed to hold his flensed gore-covered remains up.

Death stood at the cultist's side. Jacked into the dying victim was the Butcher, lost in the throes of necrophiliac bliss as he fed on those sweet agonizing final moments.

Johnny didn't hesitate for a second. He brought up his handgun and opened fire at the sick tableau. Poor a shot as Johnny was, even he couldn't miss the indulgent murderer at such a range. Sadly, the misshapen abomination had a sixth sense for danger.

Even as Johnny moved, the Butcher turned his frame-bound victim with a grunt, using the poor fool

as a human shield. Messy puffs erupted as the bullets ripped into the cultist. Johnny had to duck as
the Butcher hurled the cultist like a bloody missile.

That's when Johnny's world went sideways. His
vision blurred and his limbs felt like jelly. The pain
and fatigue from earlier penetrated even the high-
end Triad drugs still pumping in Johnny's system.
The shock-jock painfully rose to his feet, leaning
heavily on his knees.

Dammit, got to get up. Got to finish this.

Johnny groggily noticed the Butcher was in a
bad way himself. The mismatched canvas of his body
had been made even more hideous and uneven by
recent trials, chunks rent apart by gun fire. The murderer's massive bulk heaved with each billowing huff
from struggling lungs. A steady leak from the Butcher's own wounds dripped off in rivulets to join the
crimson vitae of his victims.

Johnny's fingers spasmed around his gun, ready
to fire at the creature again. The Butcher's beady
eyes narrowed to hate-filled pits at the tell-tale
twitch. With a defiant roar, the mountain of muscle
surged into the shock-jock. Johnny's firearm futilely
spat bullets, their fury wasted on the desolate room.
A giant hand closed around Johnny's neck in an un-
yielding vice, the Butcher's stinking bulk pinning
Johnny to the floor. The other hand forced a tortured
yelp from Johnny as the Butcher brutally crushed

the shock-jock's gun hand into the ground, sending the handgun clattering away. Black dots popped into life in Vid's eyes as his brain was starved of air.

The Butcher gave an excited squeal and chuckled nastily. The killer's free hand rose in a trembling rush to pluck its jack out and prepared to plunge it into Johnny's own dataport. Saliva drooled down the Butcher's puffy face at the thought of the sweet death he would savor, ending their deadly chase and finally claiming the one that got away.

A junkie getting his fix.

But the beast paused at the final moment, hunched over Johnny like a grotesque gargoyle. The giant's fist trembled around his jack, eager to taste his victim's final moments. The Butcher remembered Johnny's last trick when they'd touched minds and was content to watch the life fade from the shock-jock's eyes the old-fashioned way. Johnny struggled to push the brute off of him but his squirming did nothing to dislodge it. He punched, slapped, and clawed at the tree trunk arm crushing his throat. The Butcher snickered at his victim's antics, unmoved.

The Butcher did move, however, when Johnny's last desperate lunge connected. Mr. Vid's struggle hadn't been to dislodge the monster, only distract him. The shock-jock's jack plunged into the fat and gristle where he desperately hoped the Butcher's port ought to be. The gamble paid off as the neuro-connective cord linked with the beast's rancid cybernetics and liquid fire raced through both combatant's veins.

The cord-linked foes screamed in unison as the Brain-Eater virus gifted to Johnny by Gentleman Troung went about its business. A gruesome weapon, its creation and use carried stiff penalties across the Dynasty. The virus ate away the minds of its victims, killing the body in the process. Hearts seized, muscles tore in violent fits, and strokes cascaded through the victim, frying their nervous systems while the virus left cybernetics purged of data, but totally usable.

Slag the meat, save the metal.

The only limitation for the potent weapon was in its delivery; it needed to be inserted directly into the dataport of its victim. Johnny had infected himself, the viral-device crudely implanted into his skin, fused right into his port, so his own wetware incubated the thing, only a string of code away from being unleashed like fire.

Johnny had been warned about the pain. About the risk. Fifty-fifty odds that the virus would eat him along with the Butcher. Johnny hadn't cared about the odds. Anything to put an end to the killer's diabolic spree and get revenge for himself and the other victims of the pig-faced maniac.

Either way, Johnny would finally be free.

Free from fear of the Butcher, free from the pain of his own empty existence, free from the nightmares. At last, Johnny could escape the guilt and pain that had driven him to take refuge in other people's memories.

Take it, you monster! Feel it burn right through to your blackened soul.

For an instant, the two were connected, tethered soul to soul by a bit of cabling. Impressions hammered at Johnny; imprints of pain, fear, and grim satisfaction. The Butcher's fragmented memories washed over him like a tide. Sensory ghosts ran rampant through his brain.

For a moment, he saw the world through the Butcher's eyes.

Monsters and demons paraded everywhere. Sick, glowing, half-formed things. Johnny himself was a leering wraith, whose grinning skull mocked the Butcher. In the killer's eyes, the sadist was a warrior. A savior. A hero. To the malformed shuffling beast, his butchery purged the foulest of the foul from the planet. An offering to the siren song within him that relentlessly urged the Butcher onward, that demanded the broken creature taste his victims' ends, to devour and purify their souls, and keep killing even as pain and exhaustion dogged his every limping step.

And the worst thing. The worst thing. The Butcher hadn't always been this way.

Something, someone, it seemed to be both in the shattered recall Johnny drowned in, had twisted a mortal man into an unholy avatar of atavistic hate and rage. Memories, fragmentary and surreal, swirled about in confused eddies. Visions of otherworldly things and colors that had no definition. The only familiar rock in the torrent of life-echoes was the image of the infinity serpent and crown, held with the reverence of a holy icon. The symbol of the cult. They had taken him and molded him into a vessel for the essence of their Black Queen. They poured the need, the hunger, into the Butcher.

To know that what stood before Johnny was another's sadistic handiwork, not self-inflicted experimentation or perverse augmentation, made the shock-jock sick.

The Butcher still had to die. Whatever he had been before the cult had abducted him, the Butcher was an irredeemable killer, a broken monster. Understanding didn't diminish Johnny's hatred. It just gave it another target.

As he passed from chaotic visions to darkness, the abyss swallowed Johnny C. Vid whole.

≈

Johnny C. Vid, the man, the myth, the legend, awoke to find himself alive. Revoltingly, nauseatingly alive. His eyes burned, his head throbbed with each heartbeat, and his skin felt like it was on fire. His stomach rolled and threatened to empty itself onto the floor. It made good on that threat a moment later as Johnny puked up bile.

Eventually, inch by agonizing inch, the pain faded from overwhelming to merely agonizing. Johnny crawled to the wall and slowly dragged himself upright. The shock-jock blearily looked around the room for his nemesis. *If I'm alive, the freak can't be in a good way himself.*

Johnny didn't have to look far.

There, locked in snarling rigor mortis, lay the Butcher. The fiend lost none of his menace in death. His deformed limbs lay at odd angles, snapped and torn as stimm-bloated muscles spasmed with broken signals from a devoured nervous system. Blood oozed from its eyes, mouth, nose, and ears. The creature's final moments had been spent in fury, dents in the steel wall where it had battered its fist in helpless rage and agony.

The hateful snarl disappeared into a gory mess as Johnny emptied his reclaimed pistol into the Butcher's face. He didn't stop until the hammer clicked empty. He had to make sure.

Finally, it's over.

Johnny took scant comfort in the thought. The shadowy figures that had shaped the Butcher still roamed free. Echoes of the Butcher's profane creation still rattled around in Johnny's skull. The cultists had fled and vanished, their goals unknown but certainly sinister.

Still, Johnny lived while the Butcher was dead. Johnny could finally move on with his life. More than a living ghoul, more than a burnt-out junkie. He'd reclaimed his life from the beast and spared countless others from being taken. Johnny could face the ghosts in his dreams without fear.

The former shock-jock didn't know what tomorrow held, but he knew what he would do next.

Johnny C. Vid, the man, the myth, the legend, trudged out of the Basement to walk back to his keepers and enjoy a well-deserved rest.

Chapter 10:
Weddings, Murders,
and Other Festivities

AS HE WALKED from beneath the Basement's tunnels, Johnny's fatigued brain took several moments to comprehend what he saw in the dimly lit scrap heap.

Gentleman Troung stood, resplendent and calm amongst the twilight mountains of junk. The sight of the gold and black clad noble in the Boneyard was so incongruous, so impossible, it brought Johnny to a halt. Elder Dang stood behind the Gentleman, the crime lord's face pensive and bitter. Surrounding the duo in a tight ring stood not the Heavenly Gate Triads but something far fiercer. Starwardens, the stormtroopers of the Empress' navy, stood in a loose ring around them, professionally impassive behind reflective visors.

Even relaxed the soldiers radiated a poised lethality, looming imposingly in their midnight hued body armor and hefting humming plasma rifles.

My keepers have come to greet me. This cannot be good.

Desperate, Johnny attempted humor.

"Hello, Gentleman, Elder. Fancy running into you here. Did you come for the charming ambience or the dinner show?"

"Stay where you are and make no further gestures." The issue, crisp and merciless, snapped out from behind a mirrored plasteel helmet. Anonymous. Impersonal. Death without a conscience.

Comedy having failed him, Johnny tried to bluster his way through the situation.

"What is this? The Butcher's dead, we're safe, you don't need to..."

His voice choked off as nearly a dozen large barreled rifles pointed his way. Silence reigned until Hoa Dang spoke.

"Mr. Vid...do as they say. Please. For all our sakes. I do not wish for any more in my employ to lose their lives."

Johnny froze in place at the choking crack of Hoa Dang's voice. *Elder Dang. Afraid. More than afraid. Broken.* The implications of the mafia don's words and the sudden absence of any Triad figures chilled Johnny to the bone.

Gentleman Troung shot a reproving glance at Hoa Dang, an uncle rebuking a younger nephew for a rude tongue. "Elder Dang, please. Compose yourself. Our good servant has been through quite a trial already. We do not wish to task him further."

Having rebuked Hoa Dang, Gentleman Troung turned to Johnny and continued, calm and collected, as though their conversation wasn't being made at gunpoint.

"Congratulations are in order, Mr Vid. Your observations were quite astute. There is indeed evidence of corruption within the esteemed peerage of the Empress' Court. We wish to retain your services, so that we might utilize your talents and familiarity with these subversive elements to root out their insidious presence. To this end, we have extended an invitation to accompany us to Court. Yourself, the honorable Hoa Dang, and, of course, your friend Candace Blythe, though she will be traveling separately."

"Candace? What, why?"

"Because we are not without compassion, Mr. Vid. The esteemed news personality, Ms. Blythe, was promised an interview with Elder Dang. Alas, Hoa Dang must travel with us before he might fulfill that agreement. To honor our vassal's bargain and as a reward for your loyal services, she will be summoned to Court. We imagine this shall be much to her liking and quite a boon to her career, to be seen amongst the nobles of the Dynasty. Besides, does not a familiar face ease one's mind in unfamiliar lands?" A smile emerged that never touched Gentleman Troung's eyes.

The true reason hit Johnny like a bolt of out of the blue. *Leverage. Pressure to ensure I play along and don't bolt the first chance I get.*

"What...what guarantee do I have that you won't liquidate me like the Triads?" It took Johnny a second to force the question through suddenly parched throat.

"None. Your life is ours now, Mr. Vid. It has been since we requested your services."

The Gentleman paused as though deigning to share a great truth with an unworthy soul. "It may please you to know we did not act out of malice. Hoa Dang's outburst aside, we did not liquidate the entirety of the Heavenly Gate Triads. That would have left a power vacuum and risk entirely too much disruption to the Empress' orderly society. No, arrangements have been made with Hoa Dang's wife to run affairs in his absence as he travels with us an honored guest. The rest were simply a matter of tying up loose ends."

Of course. The fewer that know a secret, the easier it is to keep.

"What about the other Triads? They all saw you at the party."

"Indeed. We are delighted at the rumor mill that will produce, particularly as Elder Dang currently travels with us. No, Mr. Vid, we did not silence those Triads who witnessed our august presence. We merely eliminated those that heard your incautious conjecture of conspiracy at the Empress' Court. Such a slur against the Empress' perfection cannot be borne. It would undermine the Dynasty's rule and invite further insurrection." Cold eyes bored into Johnny. "Their deaths are on your hands. You would do well to still your wagging tongue in the future. It will result in many spared lives."

Johnny turned away, sickened and frightened.

"We are pleased you understand, Mr. Vid. Now, come. Our *Chariot* awaits."

The Gentleman turned as a shimmering craft descended through the murky clouds like a slow-moving comet. It would have been impressive anywhere but in the ruins of the Boneyard, the summoned vehicle's opulence was blinding. Descending from on high in a backwash of jets and humming anti-grav engines, the elegant black and golden Dynast craft alighted with a soft thump.

The Starwardens stood at attention as the flying vessel's doors silently rolled upward and a lithe figure stepped out, clothed in a black bodysuit. Bladed weapons of all kinds glinted in ripple-skin holsters at hip, hands, and thigh. Johnny eyed the newcomer warily. Though half the size of the Starwardens, the shadowed figure demanded greater fear than the host of elite warriors. The economy of movement, the lethal grace they moved with screamed that this skyborne shadow was death walking.

"The *Chariot* is loaded and cleared for orbit. We are prepared for liftoff at your word, Uncle."

"Nhi?" There was only one being that Johnny knew that would call the Gentleman "Uncle."

Though her face was covered by a visor similar to the soldiers around them, an insouciant grin colored her voice. "Hello, Mr. Vid. Good to see you with eyes of my own."

"You were stuck in the Lifeline preservation unit just a minute ago. How'd you get a body so fast?"

Nhi's amusement seemed to grow at Johnny's disbelief in her sudden resurrection. "An Assessor's duty entails many risks, Mr. Vid. We keep many vat-grown bodies on hand for just such...emergencies."

"Sure, fine, your pockets are deeper than the Enlightened One's mercy. You've got clones lying around, probably tripping over them at the office." A small part of Johnny knew he was getting flippant with some exceptionally dangerous people, but fatigue and Nhi's familiarity slowed Johnny's danger receptors until after the words left his mouth. "That I believe. But slipping into a new body isn't like changing your socks. Making those neural connections takes time and concentration." Johnny glared suspiciously at Nhi, his ire and fear finding a more tangible target than the complex machinations of a Dynasty noble, offended at yet another break in his understanding of the universe. Indignant outrage helped hold back the teeth chattering fear wracking his body. "How are you up and moving?"

"Training and discipline, Mr. Vid. Two things you are woefully unfamiliar with, sadly."

Gentleman Troung strode forward imperiously, his mere presence silencing their banter as surely as a coffin lid. "Thank you, Assessor, for your enlightening words. Yet now is the time for action. Come, honored guests. We go to Court."

The elegant flyer took off with hardly a rumble disrupting its passengers, tearing into the night sky. Johnny looked at a display monitor, watching the Heap vanish beneath him, a mountain of lights and concrete. Nausea washed over him which had nothing to do with their vertiginous ascent.

Out of the Heap and into the compactor. Johnny's eyes darted about the cabin, spacious and elegantly decorated in rich wood tones and soft gold, looking for any means of escape. Smooth visored helmet concealing her face, Nhi sat with legs folded in lotus position, seemingly in meditation. Johnny knew she more likely in communication with another party. Dang slouched next to the shock-jock, all his previous bluster, control, and even concern vanished.

Johnny tensed, prepared to leap off of the low couch seat and make a mad dash for what Johnny assumed, and desperately hoped, was the pilot's compartment, sectioned away in secure door that Gentleman Troung had disappeared through upon entering. *If I can lock myself in the cockpit, I can pilot us back down. Maybe even take Troung hostage as collateral. I just have to make it past a cybernetically enhanced combat machine to do it.*

Even as the shock-jock worked up the courage to enact the desperate plan, Nhi held up on finger. Just one. She never looked at Johnny, never changed her posture, she simply raised and wagged an index finger.

Shivering with adrenaline, Johnny took several deep breaths to slow his heart rate and arrange his jumbled train of thoughts. Then he took several more. Finally, the shock-jock ground out a question, one that kept turning over and over in his mind.

"Where's Candace?"

Nhi let out an exasperated sigh through her nose. She did in purposefully, to ensure Johnny heard and understood the depth of his ignorant question. "As the Gentleman said, Ms. Blythe will meet us at Court. Arrangements were made for her transportation from her home."

"That's not good enough. I want assurances she's okay or I won't jump. Candace is only useful as blackmail against me if I know she's unharmed."

"Contrary to your bruised ego and sense of self-worth, Mr. Vid, her invitation and transportation was a courtesy. I hardly think Ms. Blythe would have enjoyed meeting in the Boneyard with several heavily armed individuals around her. You certainly seem to resent such a rendezvous, even with a generous invitation to Court." Even behind her visor, Johnny could hear Nhi's smirk.

Deflated, Johnny leaned back in his seat and started rummaging through the wet bar in the flying luxury cruiser. He took petty satisfaction in pouring himself a generous helping of the most expensive liquor available. *Might as well make them foot the bill. Not like they can't afford it.* Contemplating the vast wealth, resources, and influence of his captors soured Johnny's short-lived joy and the shock-jock slung himself to look at his traveling companion.

"I'm sorry, Elder Dang."

Hoa Dang gave a glassy eyed shrug and shake of his head. Defeat hung on him like a pall. "Thank you, Mr. Vid, but it is not your fault. Not entirely. Fate has dealt us a cruel hand and we must abide by the judgements of the gods. Who knows? Perhaps this is my karma."

"While I appreciate your philosophical views, Elder, I fail to see what I did to deserve being abducted and swept up in Court games."

"Do not pretend your hands are clean, Mr. Vid. You sought the Triads out. You knew full well the kind of company you courted when you asked for the assistance of the Heavenly Gate. Blood would have been shed regardless. Besides, you spoke of it yourself. There are great forces at work, forces beyond us. The Butcher, those deluded fools who adore him, even Assessors and Dynasts."

Johnny frowned. "That reminds me. What the hell do these lunatics want?"

Hoa Dang barely managed a shrug. "Suffering and death, it would seem."

Johnny gritted his teeth and shook off visions of crimson vitae and ruined bodies. "Yes, thank you Elder, I understand that part. But why are they doing...what they do? It can't be for thrills." Johnny idly swirled the expensive booze in his glass, watching the ship's lights dance and play in it. "I've seen thrill killers. Even interviewed them. They love the high of the chase and snuffing someone out. Will do anything to get it. They usually act on impulse and they certainly don't share. Sociopaths make notoriously bad team players."

Elder Dang looked over-tiredly at the jabbering shock-jock. "What is the point of your musings, Mr. Vid? I prefer watching your newscasts on the Net."

Johnny rubbed his hand across his face, trying to massage away to the fugue that threatened to choke him, feeling every ache and pain in his body. The former Heap dweller's head felt like an elephant was sitting on it, trying its damndest to squeeze out every bit of grey matter.

"What I mean is that these cultists aren't doing it for the kicks. Never mind finding that many psychopaths gathered in one place is statistically improbable, they are too well organized. Too regimented. Lunatics don't usually have a dress code. I've rubbed elbows with nutjobs and crazies. Our buddies in the Basement don't synch up with that. No, these sick bastards have an agenda. I just can't figure out what."

Hoa Dang held up his hands in resignation, dismissing the matter as one of the ineffable mysteries of the cosmos, beyond the ken of mere mortals. Johnny, however, couldn't let it go. Chalk it up to the last vestiges of his journalistic training. His fatigued mind clawed and chewed at the facts, masticating them over and over. As the thoughts tumbled round and round in the shock-jock's head, something tugged at Johnny's subconscious. Two thoughts actually.

The first was that the Nhi, for all her impression of a Serene Buddha, seemed to be pointedly monitoring them and their conversation. The second was the odd subject of the cult's fervent script in the Butcher's lair. Taking a gambit, Johnny turned to the Assessor.

"Nhi, what's the Black Queen?"

As soon as Johnny uttered the words, the silence grew deeper and somehow menacing. Nhi Troung made no visible move but Johnny sensed he treaded on dangerous ground.

"A fable of diseased minds. The object of veneration for the bloody-minded cult."

"Yeah, but what is it? A thing, a person, an ideal? Their scriptures talked about it like it was something tangible. Something real. If these lunatics are killing in its name, what does it want?"

Nhi turned a mirror smooth face toward Johnny, a statue moving with glacial speed. "Intelligence is uncertain, Mr. Vid. We rarely question what a maddened dog wants, we simply put it down. Suffice it to say, it is a twisted idol. The Black Queen calls for its followers to kill in its name, to shed blood and strike down those who oppose it, to rule through fear and terror. It is the antithesis of the Dynasty's order and the Empress's enlightened rule."

Johnny had been a shock-jock for nearly three decades before his burnout. In that time, he'd talked with career criminals, politicians, and the most dishonest of scum, his fellow journalists and shock-jockeys. Johnny had swam in lies and half-truths during his career, misdirection and subterfuge had become as common as breathing. He knew when there was more to a story. Perhaps it was his numbed senses due to over-exhaustion, maybe even a delusion that he could trust Nhi, but Johnny decided to push just a little more.

"I dunno, it seemed like so much more. They talked about it...her...like she was there with them. Guiding them. Like the Black Queen was real."

A disapproving scoff echoed from the blank visor. "Murderers justifying their atrocities with fanciful tales. Such is the way of all fanatics. You give them too much credit."

Bullshit. Johnny knew stories, he knew Nhi, and he sure as shit knew when someone was ducking the question. "Most fanatics don't have secret bases and technology shiny enough to make the Dynasty stand up and take notice. They even managed to grab you, remember? There's something more to this Nhi. I can taste it."

"Mr. Vid, such line of questioning is unproductive and best not to be ruminated over. You are to heed your betters in this matter and do as is asked of you without such...ponderings."

"I don't like feeling like a pawn." Johnny mumbled to no one in particular as he slugged down his drink, relishing the burn as it went down.

The Triad crime boss leaned back with a heavy sigh. "We are all merely pawns on a board of this scale."

Johnny grumbled as he poured another shot for himself. "I seem to recall pawns always get sacrificed first."

A monofilament blade blurred past Johnny's face, burying itself into the soft leather upholstery. His burnt-out nerves shot a renewed shock to Johnny's system, cutting through the soft, comforting numb haze of exhaustion that had fueled Johnny's line of questioning. Johnny turned with wide eyes to the Assessor, who appeared to never have moved from her place of contemplation.

Johnny was starkly and abruptly reminded just how tenuous his claim to life was.

"No more drinks, Mr. Vid. Your mind must be clear for the task ahead."

Hoa Dang snatched the glass from Johnny's shaking hands and downed it in one gulp. "The Court awaits us." His hushed tones held equal parts dread and reverent awe.

Johnny shuddered. *The Court. Even at the height of my career I never thought I'd actually attend a Dynasty function.* They were as far above the Triads as the Triads were above Johnny when he'd been a burnt-out street dweller. Thinking on the sheer insanity of it made his head spin.

Each noble claimed a fiefdom within the Eight-Fold Dynasty, ruling at the behest of the Empress. They tended her realm and wielded absolute authority in their territories, countermanded only by the word of the Empress Herself. Countless souls lived and died at their command, as cities, provinces, and even planets changed hands as the byzantine hierarchy of the Dynasty shuffled with each noble's rise and fall of power. Lives were merely currency to the Dynasts, to be spent and used on a whim and to further their own Machiavellian schemes.

And Johnny was going to spy on them.

The thought should have kept Johnny rigid in fear but as he leaned back into the plush cushion, sleep overcame him, his overtaxed mind and body finally surrendering to the comforting darkness.

Johnny jolted awake with a snort, heart hammering and blood rushing in his ears. Every inch of him screamed danger. As the disoriented Mr. Vid whirled around, all he saw was the same elegant interior design, the same dejected Hoa Dang, and the same Nhi.

Though it took Johnny almost a half a minute to recognize her. Cognitive dissonance will do that to the mind.

Gone was the night black bodysheath, gleaming knives, and faceless visor. Instead, a brilliant gold and sable dress hugged her lithe form, a shimmering shawl wrapped around bare shoulders, and stocking-clad legs seen through openings on either side of the dress. *Bet it keeps her legs free in case she needs to kick someone. She looks like a totally different person out of her jet-black battlesuit. Which I guess is the point for a spy mission.*

Nhi idly flipped a fan open and closed in one hand in a dizzyingly intricate pattern while she held a small syringe in the other. A small, empty syringe. Even in the face of radical cognitive dissonance, Johnny could put two and two together.

"Did...did you just drug me? What did you put in me?" Johnny's mind churned with horrific possibilities, each more far-fetched than the next. *Dammit, please don't let it be a time release poison that the Gentleman has the antidote for! Wait, this is the Dynasty. What if it's some kind of nanite trackers or tiny bombs, ready to kill me if I step out of line?!*

Nhi watched the shock-jock squirm, seeing the fears and fantasies play out on his face.

"A cocktail of stimulants and vitamins to keep you active and attentive, Mr. Vid." Nhi's fan did an intricate dance to counterpoint her nonchalant statement and Johnny got the distinct impression he was going mocked.

"I thought you didn't like the idea of me imbibing..." Johnny cut his retort short as his rubbed at an ache in his shoulder. Something felt wrong. *Wait a minute, when did my clothes feel this...smooth?*

Johnny looked down in shock to see silk sleeves encasing his arms. The shock-jock leapt to his feet and ran to the largest monitoring, slapping it off and gaping at his reflection. Johnny stood in an immaculately pressed black and gold suit, wrought in the traditional Court style with flaring sleeves and half cape.

"You...you..." Words failed the shock-jock. "What did you do to me?"

"I removed your soiled clothes, cleaned you up, and made you half-way presentable."

Johnny closed his eyes and counted to ten. It didn't help.

"You think you have the right to do whatever you want with me? Like I'm property?"

The fan snapped shut with a harsh finality. "You are property, Mr. Vid. As am I. We belong to the Empress, our lives are her currency. I took no more salacious joy in stripping you down than I would a practice dummy or a child's toy. It is part of my duties, Mr. Vid. Infiltration, espionage, assassination. Which, as of today, are your duties as well."

At an unspoken symbol, the screen flicked online again, a stream of data pouring down the monitor. Names, titles, holdings, relations, a blizzard of information charting a web of deceit, treachery, and inbreeding.

"What is this?"

"Our weapons and our armor."

"It reads more like a gossip column in a cheap tabloid. I should know. I wrote a lot of those."

"It is what we must commit to memory if we are to maintain our cover and thus survive at Court. We must infiltrate the attendees and unearth evidence of cult activity in their amidst. Without their knowing, of course."

"Wait, so I am going to be some sort of catspaw around a bunch of freaking nobles?"

"An accurate enough description of your mission. You will serve as a distraction as well. The nobles do so love novelty. Think of it as simply one more investigative assignment, as in your shock-jock days. The nobles are only slightly less debauched and murderous than many of your other interviewees."

Johnny's eyes scrolled through the mass of data and jerked up in shock.

"Why does it say I am betrothed?"

"Because we are, beloved."

That snapped Hoa Dang out of his stupor, looking askance at the two of them.

"I suppose congratulations are in order."

Johnny's fists clenched at his side. Only his continued desire to keep breathing kept him from lashing out at his traveling companions.

"Sharing minds isn't exactly a marriage proposal."

Nhi's grin could have sent the bravest soldier running for cover. "Really? I can think of few things more intimate. Furthermore, your opinion is irrelevant. That is the cover we are using on this mission. You are my betrothed, a prospector from the edges of the Gate Worlds, recently finding some success in that warped space."

"Great, so I'm crazy as well."

Hoa Dang leaned forward fingers raised, an instructor making a point. "Let us not say crazy. Perhaps daring would be in order. All great endeavors require risk."

Johnny worked his shoulders into a tortured imitation of a shrug. "I'll try to use that as a pitch when the nobles drag me off in a straightjacket. You have to be a special kind of gutsy to brave the Gate Worlds."

When the Dynasty destroyed the Gate hub linking the Eight-Fold System to the broader Terran network during the final battles of the Glorious War of Liberation, it had devastating repercussions. First and foremost, it cut off the Eight-Fold System from the rest of the slipstream network. No longer could the former colonies rely on imports from the broader galaxy. The Sol System, cradle of mankind, could not be reached. Terra, Mars, Luna. All of them now Lost. The settlers of the Eight-Fold System truly were alone in the galaxy.

Still, the fallout extended beyond the economic and political. The damage grew to ecological and astronomical proportions as well.

The sudden release of exotic particles poisoned the galaxy for light years around. Several planets fell under the umbrella of the Gate's warping influence. Causality was bent almost to breaking and navigation proved nearly impossible in the tortured space. Instruments worked rarely and imperfectly, if at all. Strange and impossible sights occurred, ranging from ghosts of the past to the Empress Herself ranging the forsaken area.

The Dynasty sent its greatest minds to study the phenomena, quarantines were put in place, and those that could abandoned the area, leaving it virtually barren. Only the hardiest, bravest, and most idiotic of souls remained. They were called Pioneers and were often looked askance at or outright avoided by right thinking folks.

As such, countless legends surrounded the Gate Worlds, promising damnation and wonder in equal measure. Some spoke of planets made entirely of diamond. Others spoke of fleets locked in endless battle, dying, killing, and being reborn only to repeat the savage cycle. Unnumbered treasure seekers, some foolhardy and others mad, entered Gate space, hoping to find their fortunes.

Anything was possible in the Gate Worlds.

Assuming you were crazy enough to try it.

Hoa Dang continued, eyes glinting, lost in memories far more pleasant than current events. "I recall one man, Jebediah Zao, even claimed to have met his future self at the borders of the Gate's effects." The Triad crime boss paused and turned to his traveling companions, his old grin peeking through his recent perpetual gloom. "Twice."

Johnny couldn't have cared less, but Nhi imperiously waved the storyteller on with her fan. *Most animation and human engagement I've seen from her. Our dear Assessor is probably doing this just to annoy me. That or it's warmup for the Dynasty party.*

Whatever the Assessor's intent, Hoa Dang eagerly took the invitation to continue. "One tattered reflection warned him away from his quest, promising an agonizing death trapped upon a becalmed ship lost in the void, succumbing to cold and starvation as the lights dimmed and frost coated his once majestic vessel. A second apparition urged the Pioneer on, wearing finery and medals befitting an admiral. That one had urged our dear Jebediah Zao onward with assurance that wealth beyond counting was his for that taking."

Johnny quirked his head. "Wait, you said this was a Pioneer. When were you were out by the Gate Worlds, Elder?"

Hoa Dang looked offended at the mere suggestion. "I wasn't. I couldn't afford to leave my business unattended that long."

"Then how did you meet this joker?"

The former crime boss languidly waved the question away. "Oh, the good Pioneer had come back from the Gate Worlds with a modest salvage haul and was looking to barter some goods without alerting the local Dynastic authorities or paying their finders fees." Johnny buried his face in his hands and Dang seemed to notice Nhi at that moment. "Which, of course, though I entertained the hardy fellow, I would hardly have cheated the Empress of her rightful dues."

Nhi nodded, flapping an intricate code with her fan. "Very wise, Elder." She turned to Johnny pointing the fan like a dagger. "You see, Mr. Vid? You would do well to take heed of the wise Hoa Dang's example."

"How does this prove the Gate Worlders aren't insane?"

Nhi slapped her fan shut with the finality of guillotine. "Did you hear nothing Elder Dang said? Though the Pioneer was foolish enough to attempt to avoid the righteous taxes levied by the Dynasty, he earned his goods through honest work. Even the least fantastical rumors acknowledge the possibility of untapped riches in the worlds left behind. From unique minerals and specimens to salvage from intact Terran bases and derelict war vessels. Though the Dynasty's efforts to preserve remnants of history and scientific curiosities are tireless, we do not frown upon rewarding loyal citizens' initiative in bringing such things to our attention."

Despite Nhi's arguably overly idealistic portrayal of the junk-hunters, Johnny still did not like being cast in with those kind of fringe folks. *They're all a bunch of lunatics desperately chasing fables to make it rich. Grasping at straws to change their lives.* He paused, reflecting on recent events in his life. Huh. *I willingly went to the Triads to pursue revenge against an inhuman monster that tried to kill me. Shit, I have more in common with the Pioneers than I'd like to admit.*

A sudden ugly thought rose in Johnny's mind. "What if someone recognizes me from my shock-jock career?"

"Men do change careers, betrothed, and you have been gone a long time. In the lightning fast world of entertainment, you would be merely a bright star now faded. Likely only true fans, such as the esteemed Elder Dang, will remember you at a glance."

Hoa Dang, having slumped into his depressed stupor with his tale done, sat up like a child caught napping in class, nodding in blithe agreement with the Assessor's statement. "That only serves to strengthen the lie. It will also help cover your ignorance as you seek out these bands of lunatics."

"Speaking of which...what the hell are we looking for?"

Nhi spoke deliberately and carefully, as though speaking to a child. A particularly slow child. "The remains of the cult that set their temple beneath the Boneyard."

"Right, the ones that kidnapped you."

Nhi's face might have been carved from stone. Only a slight twitch on her right hand gave tell to the murderous impulse Johnny's barb inspired in her. A fact which Johnny took spiteful joy in, despite his life being at risk for the petty jab.

"Indeed."

Johnny refused to take Nhi's response at face value. "Yeah. So they had a hard on for the Butcher, got that part, but what is this business with the Black Queen?"

The black clad Assessor went statue still again, even the previous tremor vanished. "You claw at old wounds. We have told you all you need to know about the Black Queen. Cease your questions."

"Don't give me no static, Nhi. You weren't sent all the way from the Empress' Court to the Heap to scope out a simple band of loonies. Their body count wasn't high enough, and no one with money died. Not enough to get Dynastic attention."

Nhi sniffed. "You underestimate the Dynasty's generosity and concern for their citizenry. Though you are correct in one regard. It is less their physical threat and more the moral threat the cult poses. The Empress is very particular as to approved theologies. Those with ties to Lost Terra or damaging to society must be carefully pruned away."

Johnny rubbed at a growing headache between his eyes. "Please spare me the official line, Nhi. Too many people have died because of this mess for that to fly. Who or what is the Black Queen and what does the cult want?"

"The Black Queen is a dangerous icon raised by a deranged band of zealots that seek to subvert the Dynasty and disrupt the Eight-Fold system's natural order." The Assessor jabbed a finger at the glowing monitor. "Now cease your asinine questioning. We have an hour to bring you up to date on our facades and have no more time to indulge your curiosity. We begin now."

The hour passed in agony for Johnny C. Vid. Nhi was relentless, correcting any mistake, however minor, with a verbal or physical lashing. Not even Hoa Dang was exempt, expected as he was to corroborate any questions that might pertain to them. Some mistakes might be construed as Court gossip. Too many slip ups invited curious eyes. Eyes Nhi sought to avoid. As she so often reminded them, any errors could mean their untimely end.

"You are lax, Mr. Vid. I expect better from a novice, much less a famous shock-jock."

Johnny harrumphed grumpily at the mocking reminder of his former profession. "Maybe you should appreciate my position. I'm under a lot of pressure."

"It is precisely that pressure that demands perfection. Our enemies will not be so forgiving. Any mistake means death. Try again. Do better."

Johnny sighed, before un-slouching and rattling off the lengthy list of names, titles, and relations Nhi force fed him after they'd gotten him gussied up for the party.

With the monkey suit in place and rating a non-committal nod from Nhi, they'd moved on to crafting their cover story and memorizing the truly staggering amount of personal information about the party's attendees. While blessedly taking Johnny's mind off of the sheer suicidal nature of their endeavor, the minutiae drove the former journalist mad. "Isn't this a little excessive? Do we really care that the Duchess of Ca Mao's gardener plays violin on Tuesdays for The Regent of the Hou Enclave?"

Nhi's steely gaze never wavered. "The Court lives and dies by such detail and thus so do we. Now. Again."

The agonizing routine continued until a loud chime echoed in the plush room. Nhi turned to a blinking console. "Passcode confirmed, identity check secured, security clearance passed. The *Chariot* has been cleared to dock with the *Sublime Presence*.

Johnny didn't hear a word Nhi said. His eyes were locked on the external feed display, cameras projecting detailed images of the surrounding space and the singular object displayed there.

The abducted shock-jock wanted to call it a ship but such a pedestrian word failed to do the gargantuan construct justice. Johnny liked to think he'd seen some shit in his day. He'd traveled from planet to planet chasing the big and bloody stories. *I'm no provincial bumpkin, I've traveled on starships, seen orbital docks full of freighters, couriers, and even warships. But this...this is something else.*

Jet black and amber hued, shimmering with the reflected light of the sun and uncounted lights burning from within, the floating structure was cyclopean and majestic. It seemed to have its own pull, a gaudy, resplendent planet in its own right. It was three times the size of the largest battle cruiser Johnny had ever seen and that had seemed a small city in its own right. All about the floating palace, lesser craft flitted and danced about, a shoal of guardian sharks around their grand matriarch.

No, this was certainly no mere ship. The *Sublime Presence* was a symbol of the Empress' power and authority, her rule made manifest even in absentia and able to reach all corners of her realm, one part mobile base and one part roaming gala. A home away from home for the great and powerful of the Dynasty. It reminded all corners of the Eight-Fold System that the Empress' eyes were upon them. All authority descended from the Empress and the Dynasts ruled at her pleasure. Nothing of true merit could be decided without petitioning the Court. Here, entire worlds' fates were decided and the Dynastic nobles plotted and schemed under the auspices of the Empress.

Nhi smiled her killer's smile again. "Welcome to the Border Court of the Eight-Fold Dynasty, betrothed. Do try to refrain from drooling on your suit."

CHAPTER 11:
SMALL TALK AND
LITTLE DETAILS

THE INTERIOR of the *Sublime Presence* mirrored the outside, pound for pound. Coincidently, all those pounds seemed to be made out of gold. *Holy shit. It doesn't just look like a floating palace, it is a floating palace.*

In Johnny's experience, hangars and docks had universal rules; they were loud, stinking, and populated by some of the most uncouth people in the Eight-Fold System getting business done with chaotic efficiency. The *Sublime Presence* defied these conventions with wanton abandon.

The great metal cavern held ships in aligned rows like models on display in a toyshop. Not a liv-

ing soul neared the great vessels. Rather than forcing them to step onto the deck like filthy common-
ers, an air dock like a chrome snake to greet them.
Once its silvery doors opened, the burnished steel
gave way to glittering opulence, hallways bedecked
in ivory, obsidian, and gold. Marbled columns bisected mirrored panels, leading to a second door some
length distant.

Hoa Dang exited before Nhi and Johnny, two
steps behind the trailing form of Gentleman Troung,
who did not deign to acknowledge his guests' presence. The Dynastic noble expected his servants to
understand their duties and equally expected that
they be carried out.

Nhi hung back, allowing the two figures to
disappear down the long corridor before snaking
around Johnny's arm, pulling him forward.

"Betrothed, shall we?"

"Sure, just let me pull my jaw up off the floor."

A pinching sensation shot up his elbow as Nhi's
fingers found certain sensitive nerves in his arm.
Johnny worked to keep the grimace off his face.
"Dearest one, such jests are fine between you and I
but are not suitable for the Court.

"Of course, betrothed." Lowering his voice to a
harsh whisper the shock-jock hissed at his deadly
arm candy. "I liked you better when you were a brain
in a jar."

"The Butcher's flock made better companions." Nhi matched Johnny pitch for pitch, smile never fading.

Grinning like idiots, the bickering couple walked through the glittering portal to join the party.

They stepped into more opulence than Johnny had ever dreamed of.

A bewildering array of colors and designs greeted the duo. Some of it was even tasteful. Many of the assembled Dynast nobles wore bright flowing gowns or elaborate robes. Still others wore virtually nothing, showing off the finest gene-crafting money could buy, appearing as the pinnacle of fitness or other times more exotic modifications. All the finery of the Dynasty on display. Its military prowess stood at attention as well. Uniformed guards stood ramrod straight, two at every entrance, exit, and then paired more along the walls. Though dressed in parade finery, their gleaming weapons and cold gaze promised a swift death to any who discarded them as mere adornment. Johnny wasn't sure if the straight-backed soldiers were there to protect the nobles or keep the elite of the Dynasty from each other's throats.

Looking for something out of the ordinary amidst such a mountain of extraordinary seemed an impossible feat to the overwhelmed shock-jock.

"Sweet Merciful Fates, where do we start?"

"You should take the northern wing, beneath the celestial clock. I shall start by the orchestra stands."

"Wait, we're splitting up after all that happily betrothed talk?"

"I said betrothed, I mentioned nothing of happiness. We will cover more ground if we separate."

"You can't leave me like this! I don't even know what I'm looking for."

"If we knew the signs of such insurrection, Mr. Vid, it wouldn't be very a very successful rebellion. Should you need to signal me, use the body-codes we discussed in the shuttle. Do not use them without cause."

Without another word, Nhi broke off to elegantly vanish into the crowd, dark hair and crimson dress vanished behind billowing silks and gleaming holo-cloth. Left alone, Johnny mentally girded himself.

Sink or swim.

Abandoned by his keeper, Johnny mingled.

Soft music drifted in the air, played from tastefully disguised speakers, just loud enough to provide a pleasant backdrop to the murmured conversations between guests. Waiters weaved through elaborately dressed guests with platters laden with treats, coming and going from the kitchen like worker bees. Through it all, the guests smiled and made small talk.

Mind-numbingly dull small talk.

Aside from sweltering paranoia and my every move being watched, this is painfully banal. The nobles talked about nothing, petty grievances better suited to gossiping juvies and day-time soaps on the Net than the most powerful people in the Dynasty. Fortunately, utter terror kept Johnny's concentration from lapsing more than once.

He'd been idly chatting with Duchess Hon-Steiner when the slip occurred. After being regaled with the thrilling escapades of the petite duchess surviving a sloppy pedicurist, Johnny's tongue went on auto-pilot, the same snarky vitriol that served him in the office politics of the Public Eye firing off.

"You poor dear. I do hope you struggled through somehow." Eyes deader than a Triad murder-veteran turned on the masquerading shock-jock. The whole haute couture–dressed gaggle eyed the newcomer like piranhas. The Duchess' grin froze Johnny's blood in his veins. He'd seen that look on serial killers and Psyk-O stimm addicts. Both would kill you simply because they could.

Duchess Hon-Steiner turned away briefly to toss an aside to her posse. "This must be the earnest tongue of those Pioneers and Border folk so famously talked about. I am oh so glad we decided to attend this little gathering." She turned back to Johnny, that same dead-mask smile on her face. "Oh, you sweet creature. How thoughtful of you to care for my well-being. I do hope to run into you outside of Court."

The polite hope for contact sounded far more threatening than it had any right to be. Particularly from what, to all appearances, was a bored dilettante. Johnny had politely excused himself to grab something to drink, despite the full flute of champagne in his hand. He wasn't sure what kept him alive, but he knew it wasn't the Dynasts' good will.

Somehow, these people are scarier than the cultists. Johnny's journalism career, to say nothing of his recent post-career highlights, had introduced him to violence and killers of several stripes. Murderers, cannibals, torturers, he'd met and survived them all. Even shook hands and interviewed some of them. But the Dynastic nobles set Johnny's teeth grinding. *The Triads will kill you because its business. These nobles will kill you because they're bored.*

That stark realization allowed him to push past the painful small talk and pay attention.

While Johnny made his rounds, he wondered how he was still breathing. Fates, I'm wondering how anyone is still breathing. I haven't seen this much simmering resentment since the Phoenix-Tiger Gang Wars. Pretty sure I should be knee deep in rivers of blood at this point. As he contemplated this small marvel, a bit of his briefing bubbled up through the back of his mind. The Empress' Peace. A minor detail, but the reason for Johnny's continued health. In a bid to curtail the nobles' ambitions and to provide a place for negotiations and celebration, the Empress decreed that none could shed blood while in her august presence or at an event held in her name. In theory, this allowed a modicum of civility among the competing Dynastic families and oligarchs. In reality, it set the stage for delayed grudges and wars that ruined generations over petty slights at Court.

The Empress probably did it to remind them who is in charge. Besides, if she didn't provide a promise of safety, you'd probably never get all these psychopaths in one room. Which makes ruling a multi-planetary empire rather difficult. Still, I'd better be careful if I don't want to increase the list of people who want to see me dead.

As smiling faces came and went, Johnny circled through the party. Drawing on previous experience in playing nice with psychopaths, Johnny managed to not put his foot in his mouth again.

Small victories.

Finally, the shock-jock took refuge under a gleaming ice fountain, the see-through swan seeming to sweat almost as much as the frazzled former journalist. He'd survived the social gauntlet but was no closer to finding any clues about the Butcher's cult. "So, Mr. Vid. Enjoying the party?"

Johnny looked up and did a double take. The feminine voice, with its familiarity and light mocking tone, fooled Johnny into expecting Nhi. There was, after all, no one else within the floating palace that would know him. However, the woman who stood before him could not be further from his Assessor companion. Whereas Nhi was compact, lithe, and unerringly precise, this newcomer was taller, fuller, and blonder, with skin pale as the frozen statue. She was certainly more extravagant than Nhi. The blonde wore a strapless gown done in the colors of winter, accentuated by pale gold glinting at her throat and wrists. Eyes like chipped ice bored into Johnny.

"You aren't my betrothed."

A soft titter sounded out at his painful expression of the obvious. That hammered it home to Johnny. *Definitely not Nhi. Nhi doesn't titter.*

"No, but I could be if you close your eyes."

Johnny's brain came to a dead halt at the blatant innuendo. It'd been a long time since anyone had made advances on the disgraced shock-jock and recovering VR addict. Johnny's mental faculties cycled idly for a moment before his systems rerouted themselves and Johnny remembered where he was and who he was pretending to be.

"Thank you, flattered really, but I'm afraid my betrothed might object. And neither of us want that Ms.... ?"

"Call me Lavinia, my dear lamb. No need to fret. I am sure she and I could come to a meeting of the minds. Why, I feel like I already know her."

Lavinia's intense gaze put Johnny's on edge, even as her closeness sent other parts on notice. Her perfume smelled faintly of musk, an earthy and potent incense that floated at the edge of recognition. Johnny reigned himself in. *Now is not the time to be thinking about getting lucky. I know when someone's playing me.* Stepping back to a polite distance Johnny picked up a drink cooling by the ice fountain. "As I said, Lavinia, flattered, truly, but I don't think that's possible at this time."

Grin unwavering and flinty eyes dancing with silent mirth, Lavinia cocked a hip flirtatiously, the fine dress accentuating every curve. "More things exist in heaven and earth than are dreamt of in your philosophy, my dear Mr. Vid. Never discount the impossible. I have no doubt we will be seeing one another very soon."

Sauntering away, seemingly without a care in the world, Lavinia vanished into the dazzling crowd. Johnny's eyes followed her every step of the way.

Which is when he saw the mark.

Not on Lavinia, though Johnny's eyes watched her blue cloth clad anatomy very carefully, but on a noble she passed by. A laughing man in shimmering jacket of green and gold, raised a glass in mocking salute to his companions at some pithy jest or other. As the emerald sleeve rolled back, Johnny noticed something. A tiny mark on his wrist, a black infinity symbol, two snakes intertwined with a crown atop them. A mark that shouldn't exist at Court.

I know that symbol. Loud and proud in the bizarre graffiti in the Butcher's shrine. The cult's mark. Looks like they do have a man on the inside.

Eyes locked on the merry noble, memorizing his every detail, Johnny ghosted into the crowd. Swirling his drink idly under his nose, Johnny lounged against a gilded column and pretended to be mesmerized by the two-story living aquarium in front of him, entranced by the brightly colored fish swimming in the cerulean water. Nhi slid into place beside him barely minutes later, summoned by the silent signal between them.

"You've found something." It wasn't a question.

"Dynast in green. Three o'clock. The one playing happy drunk. Tattoo on the wrist holding the drink. I saw that mark in the cultists' sick tribute to the Butcher."

Nhi frowned, discreetly eyeballing the noble in question. "Jurchen Arturo-Qin. New blood, interworlds trader of middling wealth by Court standards. Primarily fine trade goods. Silks, wines, and other luxuries." Nhi's gaze swept the rest of the crowd, mimicking a moue of distaste here or an appreciative glance there, looking for all the world like a bored and vapid débutante gauging the competition. A casual onlooker would never have guessed the Assessor had recalled a Dynast noble's life story at a glance. Then again, a casual onlooker wouldn't know she was an Assessor at all.

Johnny emulated Nhi's spirited disinterest and kept his head moving as his assassin friend took another look at Jurchen's tattoo. Nhi's frown returned as she finished her sweep. "The infinity symbol and a crown. You are certain this was the cults brand? All matter of graffiti could have been splayed on the derelict walls. Some burnout might have liked the picture. For all we know it is a corporate logo or gang sign."

Johnny's calculated disdain for the party around him broke as he shook his head vigorously. He tried to play it off as shaking off a strong drink. "It isn't. Trust me. I lived in the Heap. You get to know the streets. It gets in your blood. You learn to feel its ebbs, its flows, taste its flavors. Knowing the marks of the gangs keeps you alive." Johnny sneered and had to look away from the mob of nobles. "That thing reeks of something else. Besides, I've got a feeling. Green's our guy."

The same sense of destiny that drew Johnny to the Butcher's final stand in the Boneyard tugged at him. It pointed at the man with the snake-and-crown tattoo, as surely as a compass pointing true north on Lost Terra. *Somehow, I don't think my dear minder is going to buy a gut instinct as a good enough reason to snoop on a Dynastic noble.*

The Assessor's raised eyebrow solidified Johnny's hunch as to Nhi's skepticism. Feeling his chance slip away, Johnny switched his tactics and went for an appeal to logic...and, of course, paranoia and outraged propriety. "Doesn't it strike you as odd, seeing something from that murder-cult hellhole right here, in the middle of a Dynast ball? Even if Gentleman Arturo-Qin isn't involved with those maniacs, he could be connected with elements from the Heap? Elements unsavory enough to warrant investigation, to keep him from besmirching the Empress' good name."

"A compelling argument. Move." An idiotic grin bloomed to life on Nhi's face, as unexpected as flowers in the irradiated deserts of Timbuktu.

Johnny blinked as Nhi took his arm and moved him bodily towards the exit in sudden jerking motions. *Almost like she's drunk.* "What are you doing?"

Her arms encircled his neck and draw Johnny's head down to hers, hot breath on his ear. "Taking you away for a night of passion, betrothed. And I know just the quarters for it."

Laughing with the joy of the besotted, Nhi dragged the shock-jock away from the milling crowds into the shimmering tunnels of the *Sublime Presence.*

CHAPTER 12:
PLAIN SPEAK

AFTER A BRIEF STINT of wandering the seemingly endless halls, pausing to admire disgustingly lavish décor when polite society necessitated it, and playing the drunken couple for any watching guards they happened across, Johnny and Nhi stood before an indistinct hatch, much like the one the party goers had arrived in. "How did you know where to find this?"

Nhi grunted distractedly, preoccupied with working through the door's security protocols. "I've memorized the names and ships of all the guests on board. I also happen to know where they docked, along with the layout of the *Sublime Presence*."

"Oh, is that all." *Showoff.*

Nhi's smug grin told him she knew exactly what he was thinking and agreed with it.

The door opened with a soft chime and the two darted inside to continue their espionage.

Johnny stopped dead in his tracks, awed by the sight. Rather than the gleaming opulence of the Empress' vessel, the nobles' ship looked...plain. More than that. It was bare. Spartan, even.

Sure, from the outside the ship looked large enough to suit a noble of the Eight-Fold Dynasty, but beyond that, the gleaming steel interior violently contradicted the gaudy outer covering. Coming from the Imperial court it was as different as night and day. Unvarnished metal, bolted crates, and a bed made so crisply, Johnny feared he could cut himself on it. It made Johnny's old apartment look cluttered.

After the splendor of the Dynastic party, it was a jarring contrast.

The whole thing oozed military tidiness, as anachronistic amidst the Court as it was in the madness of the Cult's Boneyard shrine and the ruined Basement laboratories. It went beyond clean. The interior was pristine, sterile, and utterly functional. Gilt, glitz, and gold wouldn't have enhanced anything in the bare ship. It just would have seemed unnecessary and cheap. Nothing extraneous existed in this orderly world.

Everything in its place and a place for everything. A surreal feeling of unease crept up Johnny's spine at the Dynast noble's quarters, the comparison to the cult's den did precious little to settle the shock-jock's frayed nerves. His certainty that the emerald clad noble was deeply involved with the cult only grew. Johnny turned to Nhi.

"Now what?"

"We look for the proverbial smoking gun, betrothed. Start searching."

A short bout of skullduggery and the duo scoured most of the ship's living quarters and bridge. It wasn't a lengthy or difficult search. Exasperated, Johnny turned to Nhi again.

"What are we looking for?"

"We will know it when we see it."

Johnny rolled his eyes at his laconic companion. "Thank you. Very helpful."

"Stop whining, betrothed, or so help me I'll stuff you into that bedspace."

Johnny and Nhi both looked at the bed latched to the floor, did a double take, and ran over to it, struck by simultaneous inspiration. With a quick pull the bed flipped up, only to reveal plas-steel storage boxes, old military grade footlockers. Johnny shook his head. He'd seen a lot of surplus military gear in his slow burn-out spiral in the Heap. They were universally cheap, easy to find, and damn near indestructible. Also, in Johnny's eyes, uniformly ugly. *You can always tell when it's military. Gunmetal, olive, and gray seem to be the colors they live by.*

"Damn." Johnny swore softly.

"Indeed."

"What now?"

"Now, I expect you to find a clue or I report to Gentleman Troung of your failure."

"Find a clue? I'm the one who found the 'clue' that got us here."

"Quite. But it led nowhere, and I have decided you require motivation to improve rather than rest on your laurels. I am now implementing that strategy. One of the perks of working with a junior partner."

Any further banter was promptly murdered by a warning chime from Nhi's databand, a hyper-advanced bit of tech masquerading as an understand obsidian and gold swirled bangle. The proximity sensor they'd placed in the hallway had been tripped and the bio-metrics matched those of one Jurchen Arturo-Qin, whose ship they were currently traipsing through like a couple of sneak-thieves. It seemed the Dynast noble was coming back to his quarters.

"Hide!"

Johnny frantically scanned the vessel, looking for some way to hide two humans in the barren space. A bit of a challenge since you couldn't have hid a dime-bag of Dream-Dust in the squeaky-clean ship. "Where?!"

The duo looked at each other and wordlessly came to an agreement. Jumping into the storage space, they wedged themselves between the footlockers, slamming the fold out bed on top of themselves.

The door chimed open only a few panicked heartbeats later.

Please don't be laying down for a nap. Please, please! Johnny's silent litany suddenly changed as a horrifying thought struck him. *Oh crap. Please don't have a date!*

Their unknowing host slid brusquely over to the communications panel and fired it up, the ubiquitous pinging noise that all devices gave on startup alerting the hidden eavesdroppers. Without even waiting for an answer, Jurchen began speaking into the device, his tone firm and his voice clipped, sounding for all the world like a military debriefing.

"Boneyard mission and base compromised, house-guest is free and in the wild. We no longer have eyes on the house-guest. Confirming secondary package remains in play. Repeat, the Lamb is still active though uncontained. Report status on your end." A moment of silence, as the noble apparently listened to someone on the other end. Judging by the scoff and snarl that reached the two eavesdroppers' ears, Jurchen did not like what he heard.

"Not my problem. I don't care how many of you it takes, get it done." There seemed to be some backtalk from the other end, as Jurchen snarled and swore in a manner very unbecoming of a refined Dynast noble. "Congratulations on discovering how imminently expendable you are, you pathetic copy. This is exactly what you were made for. Clean up the mess and secure the second site." Another moment of silence punctuated by the Dynast's frustrated hiss. "Yes, you addled half-wit, the asylum." Slamming the machine off, Jurchen moved away, his cursing fading. "Damned Newbloods. May the Queen take all second-generation knockoffs."

No sooner did the door chime than Nhi and Johnny shoved free of their padded prison. Both dashed to the console, jacks flying toward the port. They froze mere moments from colliding, both jacks poised for the console, looking at one another in irritation.

Nhi gently moved Johnny's jack out of the way. "Betrothed, leave this to me."

"Not a chance, the Butcher is mine." Johnny held firm, though it took a bit more effort than he'd expected.

Nhi's second push was far less gentle and sent Johnny staggering a step, proving the quality and potency of the finest bionic and cybernetic augmentations within Dynastic space. "This could be military grade encryption, you are ill equipped to handle it."

Johnny pushed back at the stiff arm at his chest, which proved as easy as wading through wet concrete. "I'm an old hat at this."

"I know. That is the problem." Bodily shoving the shock-jock aside, Nhi jacked into the port.

"Did...did you just imply that I'd relapse by downloading at a console?"

Nhi didn't answer, mind delving into the on-board computer, tracing coordinates through what Johnny assumed was layers of encryption, false-files, and enough counter-measures to slag an uninvited hacker's brain.

Furious, Johnny turned to watch the sterile room. Which meant he came face to face with the good Arturo-Qin walking back through the door. The noble looked quite stunned to find a strange man standing in his bedchambers.

Without a word, Johnny snagged Jurchen by the shirt, head butting the noble as he went. Which instantly sent jolts of pain through Johnny's skull. *Sonuvabitch, that hurt! Always works in the flicks.*

Even as he reeled, the green clad noble whipped a small dagger from his back and lunged at Johnny. Even through the bulky formal Dynastic party getup it was clear the Gentleman knew what he was doing. The movements were crisp, fluid, full of murderous intent. The knife flashed toward Johnny quick as a snake.

Fortunately, the shock-jock's legs were longer than Jurchen's arms.

Reflexes from his days in the Heap kicked in and Johnny's borrowed expensive footwear connected with Jurchen's family jewels. As soon as the man and his knife went down, Johnny pounced, frenziedly battering at the noble's head until he stopped moving.

Panting, Johnny fell back onto the bed, gingerly cradling his bruised and bloody knuckles.

"I hope you didn't kill him. He is a Dynast, after all."

Johnny jerked in reflex, only to see Nhi looking directly at him, still plugged into the system.

"Gods preserve me, Nhi, you nearly gave me a heart attack." Johnny nudged the prone figure with his foot, who promptly groaned. "Not to worry. The Gentleman's alive. Going to have one hell of a hangover though."

"Good. He must live to face the Empress' justice."

"I'm fine by the way, thanks for asking."

Nhi didn't even bother to shrug. "You are clearly unharmed in any meaningful way, betrothed, and thus there was no reason to inquire."

"Wonderful." Johnny stood up even as Nhi lithely stalked over the nobleman to the exit. An ugly thought struck him on the way as the adrenaline subsided and rational thought took over.

Nhi was aware of her surroundings even in deep dive with the computer. Grudging respect oozed side by side with irritation. *She only pretended she couldn't hear me to dodge my questions.*

"So, the whole locked in the computer and can't hear me thing? Faking the whole time, huh?"

"I'm an Assessor, betrothed. It is what I do."

Coordinates stored securely in Nhi's magnificent cyber-brain, the duo canoodled their way back to the *Chariot* in the way of besotted loving couples throughout the galaxy. Clutched tightly to one another in amorous embrace, it helped hide Johnny's bloody knuckles as his hands roamed beneath Nhi's tasteful evening attire.

The act was made decidedly less lascivious by the throbbing pain of Johnny's injured hands, the knowledge that Nhi could and would kill him six different ways if he overstepped boundaries, and the presence of an armored body sheath beneath the dress.

Flexible but durable, the plexi-steel material could deter knife, club, and even provide some protection from fire and electricity. It was a stark reminder that the Assessor came prepared for violence and mayhem, no matter how pleasing a mask she wore. In short, Johnny's hands moved less out of the thrill of it and more out of a need to maintain their charade.

Now and again, his hands would graze the slim armor and send a shock of pain through his wounds. A leer on Johnny's face turned any grunt of pain into a licentious act. *That the armor slaps me in the face with exactly what sort of world I'm living in now is simply incidental to the act of me still breathing. I suppose I'll be getting more reminders, assuming I live long enough. Perks of the job, I guess.*

Once within the security of their gleaming safe house, Nhi dashed to a terminal and instantly began downloading the purloined data. Johnny helped himself to the med-station built into the Dynastic vessel. Unsurprisingly, the sleek craft's medical supplies proved as well-stocked as its bar. No sooner had Johnny placed his bloody and aching hands into the sink than the advanced bio-computer began its work. Blue rays shot out, tracing his injured digits and analyzing Johnny's injuries to the cellular level. Tiny screens blipped on, scrolling rolls of data that meant nothing to Johnny but would probably have described the cause, symptom, and cure for whatever ailed the shock-jock to whoever knew how to read it. *Dammit, I'm a shock-jock, not a chop-doc or body-fixer!*

Fortunately, the system was idiot-proof and even as Johnny squinted as the scrolling data, a host of maniples, tiny robotic arms, erupted from hidden alcoves and descended on his hands. In a flurry of motion, Johnny was cleaned up, wounds dressed in synth-skin, and numbed with anesthetics so refined, he barely felt a tingle.

Can't even feel the pain and I'm still walking straight. That is some quality stuff. It'd go for a fortune back at the Heap. Johnny experimentally flexed his hands, clenching and unclenching his fists and running his fingers like a star synth-chord player at their keys. *Everything checks out fine. Damn near good as new.*

The onboard computer was apparently quicker on the uptake than its patient, the many medical instruments receding into their protected alcoves once their duty was discharged. In seconds, the port simply looked like any other sink in a bathroom or wet bar.

Still playing with himself, Johnny and his newly minted digits wandered over to where Nhi sat, cross legged, digging through the data they had purloined from Jurchen Arturo-Qin.

"Anything?"

"Mr. Vid, I am an exceptionally talented Assessor and am fully capable of cutting through the deepest encryptions and parsing the densest information. However, it is still not instantaneous. Additionally, such endeavors proceed much faster without the outside world intruding with senseless questions."

Johnny held up his newly patched hands. "So sorry, honored Assessor. I figured after your brilliant multitasking while I had a duel to the death with a Dynast noble belonging to a secret murder cult you could have cracked this little code with nary a sweat."

"Allegedly belongs to a murder cult, Mr. Vid. As I said, I am talented, and it is a particular talent of mine to ignore minor irritants and unimportant matters."

"You are a joy to work with, Assessor Nhi."

"Quite. The same might be said of you, Mr. Vid."

Silence reigned in the *Chariot* as Nhi went about her work and Johnny sulked. Minutes ticked by as Nhi parsed and sorted data, seeking the trail of the cults. Suddenly, Nhi rose and turned to her companion. Johnny jumped a step back at the sudden motion. He barely tracked what happened. It was like watching a snake uncoil, a puff of smoke change shape, or a vid-scene skip. One-minute Nhi was sitting, the next she stood facing him with eager intensity.

I know that look. I saw it in the mirror a lot in my shock-jock days. Hunger. She's got a lead.

"I have them. Our coordinates lead to the Tranquil Moons Preserve, a tract of untouchable nature held in part by the Arturo-Qin estates. In exchange for this honor, they are permitted to operate a hunting lodge and villa amidst the pristine wilderness."

The news did not cheer Johnny in anyway.

"Which means no easy transport in, no easy way out, and no witnesses to corroborate our untimely demises."

"Precisely."

"And we still have to go there."

"Correct."

Johnny grunted sourly. "Wonderful."

"Such is the duty of an Assessor, Mr. Vid. Do try and cope."

Even as Nhi and Johnny argued, the *Chariot* smoothly sailed from the confines of the *Sublime Presence* and edged out into open space. Stars soared by on the external monitors but the shock-jock paid it no mind, the over-tired Johnny unsuccessfully attempting to convince Nhi to call off the suicide mission.

Johnny only noticed they had left for open space when a chime rang throughout the cabin. A ship blocked out the light on the monitors. He turned and blinked, shocked to see they were heading right for it, its bays open and docking lights blinking. It gleamed like a dagger of shadows hanging in space, long and sharply prowed. This was a hunting vessel, an arrow, to fly straight and true towards its prey.

"What in the hells is that and why are we heading towards it?"

"Our quarry is some distance from us, Mr. Vid. The *Chariot* is a fine vessel, but is hardly equipped to travel between planets. The *Cheng I Sao* is more than capable of getting us to our target." A savage grin erupted onto Nhi's face. "More importantly, it will get us there swiftly and unseen. They shall never see the blade until it is in their ribs."

CHAPTER 13:
FALSE FACES

STEPPING INTO THE DOCKING BAY of the *Cheng I Sao* was a welcome return to normality for Johnny C. Vid. The glitz and impossible tech of the Dynasty fell away, traded for sights and smells Johnny had known for decades. Overall-clad workers ran to and fro, barking orders as they went about the innumerable and inexplicable tasks that kept a starship running. Exhaust, oil, and sweat suffused the area with a gentle musk that brought the shock-jock back to his days in the Heap.

Johnny didn't trust it for an instant. He couldn't. Not while Nhi sauntered across the busy floor looking utterly at ease. It was clearly home turf to the Dynast assassin. *If Nhi is comfortable, that means something else is going on.*

A tall, dusky woman in white breeches, boots, and severely cut jacket, the ubiquitous uniform of a civilian spacer officer, stood at attention by the door. She carried herself with an air of authority that left no doubt this was the captain of the *Cheng I Sao.* A heavy-set fellow loomed behind her like a husky shadow, barely fitting into his own pearl uniform. His craggy features never shifted from a perpetual frown, eyes bouncing from a data-slate made dainty by his large hands to the many moving bodies in the bay. As Johnny approached, he was struck by the captain's eyes. Her right was a cloudy green, almost jade. The left eye was an obvious prosthetic, black and gold shifting cybernetic lenses intensely gazing at everything around the mistress of the vessel.

Nhi strolled within arm's reach of the imposing duo and gave a small bow, the polite gesture marred only by the sneer on Nhi's face. "Captain Ezra, thank you allowing us to board your fine vessel. I am sure the cooked rat that passes for rations on board this rusty tub is delicious as ever."

The captain leaned forward, artificial eye twisting and zooming as she came within inches of the Assessor. "It's still too good for you, you prissy little shadow-skulker."

The two glared for two seconds longer before breaking into hearty laughs. Which gave Johnny's heart permission to beat again.

"Truly, Esmerelda, thank you for abandoning your current expedition to aid us." Nhi gave an earnest nod.

"Always happy to serve Her Sublime Majesty, Nhi. Always." Her prosthetics swiveled to Johnny. "Who's this?"

"A soul fortunate enough to be of immediate value to the Dynasty and the Empress. Captain Ezra, may I introduce Johnny C. Vid, my current charge and vassal to House Troung in service to the Dynasty. Mr. Vid, know you have the honor of addressing Captain Esmerelda Ezra and her First Mate, Denton Boji. You will treat them with the utmost respect, for they are unsung heroes of the Dynasty."

Johnny bowed low, taken aback by the pride in Nhi's voice. *She respects them. Hell, she knows them. They came at Nhi's beck and call. I knew there was more to this than some mid-level courier ship.*

Underneath the weathered and professional exterior, Captain Ezra seemed embarrassed by the praise. As she moved to wave off the compliments, Johnny could see the prosthetics went far deeper than just an eye. Muscles moved stiffly, flesh pulled tight or bulged when augmetics moved beneath it. The captain handled it well, but it was clear that there wasn't much of the original biology left under the uniform. The mere thought of the damage made bits of Johnny's anatomy shrink in sympathetic pain.

Captain Ezra has seen some serious shit and lived to tell the tale.

"We all serve, Assessor, to the best of our abilities. That's all there is to it. Now, you mentioned a bit of sensitive data. Let's retire to my quarters and see what we can do with that little gem." The captain turned to her first mate. "Boji, get the crew sorted out for immediate departure. I want the *I Sao* ready for full burn in twenty minutes. As of now, we are on the hunt."

Boji snapped off a crisp salute. "Yes, Captain. I'll have them ready in ten."

"Good man. Now, Assessor, if you please."

As Nhi and Captain Ezra headed for a nearby door, Johnny moved to join them only to find his way blocked by a wall. A wall named Boji.

Johnny darted a quick glance between Nhi, Captain Ezra, and the current obstacle in his way. "Nhi?"

"Your services are not required at this time, Mr. Vid. The good Mr. Boji will assist you in getting settled while I discuss the data with Captain Ezra. Once we have formulated a plan, we move on our target. Do not get too comfortable, this will not take long. What you do until then is of little concern to me."

Considering the matter settled the two turned and moved beyond noisy docking bay, vanishing behind a metal door.

Muttering to himself, Johnny looked at the dour First Mate. "So, what's the plan?"

"The plan is that you get out of the way. I've got a ship to run."

"Sure, fine. Sounds good. Say, you mind if I use the can?"

"I don't give a damn. Just keep the hell out of our way."

Boji began barking orders, directing the chaotic flow like a conductor at an orchestra. Johnny watched with fascination at the efficiency of the crew. *They could put an assembly line shame.*

Faced with a potent combination of frenzied activity and placid indifference, Johnny ducked through the same door as Nhi and Captain Ezra to avoid being trampled underfoot by the relentless crew. Making himself scarce, Johnny set off deeper into the ship.

For over an hour, Johnny traversed hallway after hallway of the *Cheng I Sao*, ducking and dodging crew as they bustled about on inscrutable missions. At first the shock-jock apologized profusely for getting underfoot but by the twelfth time the spacers shouldered by him, Johnny met the crewmembers scowl for scowl. *Oh, am I in your way? Sorry, I was dragooned by an Assessor, abducted from a planet, and sent on a Black Ops mission. What's your excuse?*

Johnny ducked, dodged, and dove to get past the bustling foot traffic clogging the tight corridors, trying to lose himself in the bowels of the courier vessel. *How many people are on this tub? It's not that freaking big!*

The more Johnny wandered the *I Sao*, the more he realized how much more to the courier there was than first met the eye. They hid it well, but Johnny kept noting the little things. In his experience, the little things often kept you from getting dismembered.

Time and again, civilian crew members moved with military precision, flashed hand signals like gang speak from the Heap, and more than once Johnny swore he saw high level encryption flying past a work console moments before the crewman manning it flicked it over to standard ship schematics.

Which happens as soon as they notice me. Of course. I knew I'd entered the Assessor's world of secrets and shadows...I just didn't expect it to run so deep. Johnny wondered just how many pleasant facades held darker truths. As a former journalist, he felt deeply intrigued and more than a little offended he'd never noticed.

Finally, Johnny found a quiet corridor, the only sound the humming of the engines and the light buzz of fluorescent lights bolted into the ceiling.

Nothing but empty bulkhead stretched out in either direction, turning sharply at both ends.

Finally, a moment of peace. No cleaver wielding maniacs trying to kill me, shoving me around at gun or knife point, or forcing me into skullduggery. I know it's just the old VR flickers bouncing round my skull, but feels like I should light up a cig, even if I don't smoke. Fits the ambience. Wonder if I'm the hardboiled detective or the survivor after the big battle.

Johnny sat down, closed his eyes, and leaned against the bulkhead, enjoying the isolation.

This regrettably lasted less than five minutes when he started hearing voices from the air.

"Hey, buddy, you mind moving? I can't get out of here with your fat ass in the way."

Johnny shot up like he'd been launched from a cannon, not expecting to hear someone talking from *under* him.

A section of the floor popped up, virtually invisible until it sprang open with a clang. Out of the newly made hatch climbed a female crewmember covered in grime, coveralls more oil, dirt, and burned patches that clean cloth. Short, stocky, and tattooed, the technician seemed an extension of the ship itself. She pulled herself free with a grunt and dragged a small utility pouch after her before shutting the hatch with a clang. The opening vanished as if it had never existed, looking like just another unremarkable patch of corridor. Without wasting a word, the pop-up technician parked their rear on the newly resealed floor, fished out a bent cigarette, and lit up. A sigh of relief rose into the air alongside a cloud of pungent smoke.

Johnny waved the cloud away with a sneeze. *Glad we got that ambience out of the way.* Silence reigned in the corridor as the crewmember enjoyed their smoking stub, only the rhythmic inhale and exhale sounding out like a nicotine tinted breathing machine.

Johnny tried to get a read on his laconic neighbor. *For example, will they try to stab me, abduct me, or enact a grudge potent enough to wipe out a quarter of a planet's population after five minutes of small talk?*

Given the grime encrusted crew member's complete refusal to acknowledge Johnny's presence, much less engage in any form of chit chat, Johnny ruled out the latter pretty firmly. Faced with half a cigarette left and zero response, Johnny took the initiative.

"Hey there, nice to meet you, name's Johnny."

The seated figure ignored Johnny's proffered hand and didn't so much as look at the shock-jock as she replied. "Johor."

Ah, okay then. No sweet talking here. Direct approach it is.

"So, what do they have on you?"

"What?" There were a lot of ways to say a word, but Johnny had never before encountered one that conveyed an extended narrative of disapproval and warning of beatings at further inquiry in a single syllable.

"What do they have on you?"

"What makes you think anybody's got anything on me? It's called a job, dirtsider. Three hots and a cot and enough spare change to make surface-leave interesting. That's it." Johor glared up at Johnny through a bandanna that might have been red once but was so filthy it looked maroon.

Real scary, tough gal, but you aren't even the third scariest thing to threaten me this week. "Because the pirates of the Red Dwarf Band don't go straight unless some serious shit went down." Johnny pointed at the stylized crimson sun burst and dagger tattoo on the tech's arm, peeking out from a layer of grime and the sleeve of the coverall. "Since you're here, working for a captain that's on friendly terms with an Assessor of the Eight-Fold Dynasty, I'm guessing they have some serious dirt on you."

The burning stick hung smoking like a stick of incense at a temple, as the former pirate glared like an angry guardian-statue at the talkative shock-jock who quickly held up his hands in the universal sign of "don't punch me, I'm just saying."

"I'm not making any judgements, and I don't need all the sordid details. The Dynasty has me by the short and curlies as well. Just trying to see how other folks got roped into this business."

"They don't have a damn thing on me. Not anymore."

"You're screwing with me."

Johor sat back and stared at the corridor walls, lost in memory. "Nope. Yeah, I ran with the Red Dwarf Band. We were the scariest sons of bitches to ever ply open space. Even had the Dynasty quaking in its boots. I've scuttled ships, taken plunder and captives, spaced more souls than I care to admit. Then, my crew got sloppy. Got caught. Long arm of the Dynasty caught up with us. Made a good fight of it, but you know how this story ends. They gave me a choice; serve or die." The cigarette bobbed and moved with the story, rolling back and forth as the tale poured out of the starfarer. "Seeing as all my comrades were dusted, I figured why the hell not. I'd escape eventually. They stuck me with the Captain."

The techie took a deep drag of the cigarette, smoke rising from her like a dragon of old myth.

"I watched Captain Ezra risk life and limb for us time and again. Even if we didn't deserve a damn bit of her faith in us. She braved hell itself and came out the other side in the name of the Dynasty, Empress, and the crew. And I've walked those damned miles right beside her. I've seen horrors you couldn't even name."

"Try me."

Johnny met the technician's stare and held it, shared pain and old terrors echoing in their eyes.

"Heh. Maybe you could. Seems you've seen some shit yourself. Makes sense, I guess. No one gets here by being a saint. Maybe you'll understand."

"Understand what?"

Johor passed the half-used cigarette to Johnny, the two slouching against the bulkhead like juvie-delinquents.

"Damn near all of us started out the same way. We all got into the life one way or the other but it boiled down to the same thing. Abducted. Blackmailed. Cut off from everyone and everything we ever knew. But we're all here because we choose to be."

"Maybe. Or maybe it's because you are too damaged and got nowhere else to go?"

Before the technician could respond, the ship's intercom chimed and Nhi's clipped voice rang in the corridor. "Mr. Vid, attend to the Chariot at once. Captain Ezra has set us underway and we shall arrive at our destination in but a few hours. I would have you prepared for the mission. That is all."

Johnny paused, mouth agape, cigarette nearly falling to the floor. "Arriving in few hours? But, even

Kadath is half a day out. How can we reach some mudball out in the middle of nowhere that fast? It's impossible."

The shock-jock glanced over at Johor, who simply shrugged, looking inordinately smug. *I've seen the Assessor use some impressive tech. Bleeding edge stuff. But this...this shouldn't even be possible. I know the Dynasty Nobles lived in different worlds. Had shinier, better, cleaner toys than any of us lowly commonfolk. But this isn't about toys, this is about physics. Nothing moves this fast!*

Johnny turned with arms extended and an exaggerated look of shock on his face, hoping his non-verbal shout was loud enough for his laconic companion.

Apparently, it was. "Not possible, right? That's what the Dynasty wants you to think. I told you, Johnny boy, I've seen some shit. We have some pretty amazing toys here. Beyond cutting edge. But best keep your lips shut. Don't want to give the little people any ideas. If they knew how advanced it could get, they might try to grab it for themselves. Safer to keep them in the dark. Better that way."

"Better for who?"

"Everyone. Well, okay, the Noble bastards mainly, but really all of us. I've stood between the impossible and the common folk enough times to be very careful about letting certain knowledge into the wild. I don't fancy seeing another planet have chunks torn out of it because some yahoo tried duplicating a singularity-drive."

"A what?!"

Johor punched Johnny once in the shoulder with a smirk and gathered up her toolkit. "Working for the Dynasty will make you a believer. It did for all of us." Before leaving, the technician turned over her shoulder. "We're all damaged, Johnny. Find comfort where you can. Else you'll be blowing your brains out in two weeks." Cheerful nugget of wisdom passed on, Johor turned 'round the corner and vanished from view.

Johnny looked down at the cigarette burning away between his fingers before taking one last drag and departing to meet with the esteemed Assessor Nhi and jump into the jaws of almost certain death.

CHAPTER 14:
A CRADLE AND A GRAVE

NHI HAD NOT EXAGGERATED the *Cheng I Sao's* speed. The unassuming ship hovered above the Tranquil Moons Preserve, a silent judge, ready to dispense vengeance and justice upon the world below. The verdant orb hung in the *Chariot's* monitors like a picture framed at an art gallery.

"Chemical burns and fission-wakes, all around the area. For a distant and unpopulated world, the amount is unprecedented, indicating recent heavy traffic of between planet's surface and orbit."

"Jurchen's message?"

"It seems likely. With luck they have already left."

"And if not?"

The playful grin returned to Nhi's face. "Then as one of the Forgotten Faiths' oaths say, until death do us part, betrothed."

"Don't we have a host of Starwardens floating aboard this thing? Surely they can handle this? We point them in the direction we think the cultists are and let them do their work."

"No, Mr. Vid. This vessel is designed for stealth. Its crews' talents lay in subtler fields. This is our task. Not theirs."

"My talents lie in subtler areas as well, Nhi."

Her grin returned, feral as ever. "Then what better time to grow your new talents. Consider it on-the-job training."

"Job? I was abducted, dragooned, and blackmailed into this. What exactly am I being paid?"

"The highest currency of all, Mr. Vid. You are being allowed to live. Now, cease your prattle and follow me. Vengeance will be ours."

≈

Johnny crept through the dark undergrowth, shadows deepened by the twin moons above. Silver and sable defined his world. Nhi stalked ahead, one more shadow amid countless others.

The lodge had been easy enough to find. Cresting a hill with delusions of mountain-hood, it gave a commanding view over the tree line for a fantastic vista of the wilderness below. Nature, pristine and untouched, spread as far as the eye could see.

Having lived in the Heap for his entire adult life, Johnny didn't care much for the place. *Bunch of trees and rocks, so what? Just makes it harder to reach the damn place.*

They'd set the *Chariot* down some miles out, coming in cold and barely using silent retros and inertial dampers to soften then meteoric descent at the last moment. Apparently the ostentatious hunk of metal could do stealth mode as well. *Who knew?*

Now, nearing the end of the uphill, several mile hike, Johnny swore off camping. Forever. *I only promise myself I won't ask "Are we there yet?"*

In truth, Johnny kept his bluster inside because he didn't dare make a sound. The shock-jock could feel the hairs on the back of his head stand up. Everything was too quiet. In the Heap, there was always noise. Always people. The only animals were rodents, winged and otherwise, and stray pets. The biggest predators walked on two legs and made sure you knew who owned the area.

Small wonder then, that the stillness of the shadowed woods unnerved the shock-jock.

Last time it was this quiet, I got impaled by a pig-faced freak with a necro-fetish.

The gentle touch on Johnny's arm nearly made him scream. The lighting-fast hand clamping his jaw shut stifled that plan.

"Mr. Vid. I have found a way in." Johnny thought the whispered words carried a hint of reproach. *Though I might be projecting a bit due to the choke hold.*

Creeping stealthily, they came to a side gate, some sort of quaint servants' entrance, covered over with ivy. Nhi had already dealt with the lock. Within, a broad open pavilion greeted them, the very picture of stately provincial decorum, emphasis on "picture." The whole thing felt staged, from the wreaths pinned to wooden paneling in the styles of Lost Terra, to the slightly rusted barrel rings stashed in the corner. The house held an air of artificiality that worked at a distance but whose façade fell away up close.

Pretty sure I saw this in a postcard at a Kwiks-Mart.

The entrance lay open, cobble and concrete ramp leading to a sliver of darkness, the wood and glass panel hanging ajar. Johnny and Nhi slipped in without a sound. The two crept through the deserted lodge, the mansion like building's dark wooden interior granting it an oppressive and ominous air in the quiet night. *Reminds of those old schlocky horror vids. We just need some organ music playing.*

Everywhere were signs of hasty retreat, much like the Boneyard minus the bleach and bullet holes. Disorder marked the spacious mansion. Drawers and cabinets hung open, revealing bare cupboards. Absent furniture stood about among the staged décor like missing teeth. It seemed the cult had mastered the art of a rapid getaway.

At last, they followed the trail of ransacked household goods to a blank hallway, an empty bedroom to their right and a bathroom on the left. So ordinary and unremarkable it set Johnny's paranoia sky rocketing. *I remember Tricky-Fingers Luke always telling me how the smart marks didn't put their jewels in the big safe. They kept the good stuff hidden away in plain sight.*

Johnny knelt and examined the floor, fingers trailing along ugly scuff marks. He risked some light and fired up the flashlight, shining it over the floor. *No break in the scratches. Something big got dragged right into the wall.* Reaching up he pulled on one of the lighted sconces illuminating the hallway. True to form, it moved with a soft click, revealing a hidden door. *Horror vid cliché. Gotta love the classics.*

The feeling of déjà vu intensified as Nhi and Johnny descended into the dark, flashlights out and piercing the gloom. As with the underground lair in the Boneyard, beakers and wires hung about the looted laboratory, half-abandoned technology shoved into corners in the narrow walkway. Even the plain, dull, unimaginative grey, olive, and brown mirrored the foul pit on distant Kadath.

Only one key difference mattered. Past gurneys with worrisome looking straps and inset drains in the bare floor, Assessor and company found the beating heart of darkness lurking beneath the lodge; a central mainframe. Military drab like the other equipment, the large rectangle looked down at an operating theatre. All around Johnny and Nhi, burned papers lay in ashen piles. File cabinets spilled charred guts. The room reeked of oil and smoke, burnt offerings to the gods of lies and secrets. Before Nhi could protest, Johnny slammed his jack into the computer.

"Mr. Vid!"

"The Butcher hung me up like a side of beef and tried to turn me into his private snuff film. The pig-faced freak racked up a sickening body count, and we have a chance to stop the sick bastards that wound him up and let him loose. I. Got. This."

For a moment, Nhi stood poised to violently yank Johnny away from the computer, but instead oozed back into the shadows.

Rummaging about the damaged mainframe's files, Johnny snorted in disgust. "These lunatics were sloppy as shit. Reeks of a rush job. I'm willing to bet they hit delete and thought that was that. Except with these babies that's not good enough. Nuh uh. Unless you break the thing, nothing's really gone. Especially with big sturdy bastards like this." He brought his hand down on the console with sadistic glee. "Haven't seen anything this durable in a while. Would have made the Empress' Starwardens' proud, back in the day. Thing's old but sturdy. My favorite kind of computer to snoop through. I've gotten more than one scoop on dirty politicians by digging through these hulks. These things usually have firmware built in to back it up. You know, to make up for general human laziness...Ah! There!"

Fragments of data started to stream by the screens, even as it flowed into Johnny's mind. His eyes flickered behind half closed lids, taking the torrent in and piecing it together.

Two seconds later Johnny wished he hadn't. The shock-jock flinched as the full, monstrous scope of the cult's actions unfolded. The faces, and the remains, of men, women, children, raced by, often accompanied by fragmented reports documenting the nightmares inflicted on them. The cold sterile descriptions of acts depraved enough to make the most jaded Heap dweller blanch made it even worse. Though incomplete and half coherent, the images were monstrous, the data terrifying in its implications.

"Those sick fucks. Abductions, falsified reports, bribes, murder. There's enough here to drag in a quarter of the Court officials across the Eight-Fold System." His eyes flicked unseeing through report after report of inhuman experiments. "They've got their claws in deep. Churches, orphanages, asylums. Anywhere they thought they could get away with it and no one would ask any questions. Shit, I've stayed at a few of these places! Nhi, this isn't new. They've been doing this for years. The sick shit they're pulling off, they have it down to a damned science. It's practically routine. Wait. Hang on. Oh, Merciful Fates."

Johnny pulled up short, his attention halted entirely by a small report, one of the oldest. Little of it remained but the incomplete report told of repeated therapies, tortures really, disguised as a healing treatment. Some poor bastard had volunteered for the doctors' tender mercies, fed sweet lies, believing the treatment would help him. The scientists had been trying to recreate something, a potent weapon of some kind, to turn this hapless man into a prototype. It worked. All too well. The still security feed images showed a shadowed giant of a figure, tearing into the staff and guards with gusto, before fleeing the asylum.

The last frame showed the mammoth creature in clear resolve; a mismatched slab of muscle with a grinning pig mask covering his face.

"The Butcher." The monster wasn't as big as when Johnny knew him, but there was no mistaking the abomination for anything else.

"Yes, our finest mistake."

Johnny whipped his head out of the computer, cord snapping back, feedback-tension nearly doubling him over. In Johnny's blurry vision, Jurchen Arturo-Qin's double images walked calmly into the room, festooned with a bulging sack. Seemingly without a care in the world, Jurchen methodically attached explosives throughout the room. "He was magnificent, you understand. Physically durable but wounded within. A pliant, willing mind. A trusting vulnerable soul. And we took that and remolded it into something so much more. A perfect vessel for the Black Queen's Gift."

Johnny lifted his aching head to glare at the Dynast noble, all shifting two of them. "Black Queen? You mean that pretty little fairy tale you crazies' worship?"

Jurchen looked at Johnny with an offended scowl. "The Black Queen is very real and alive within us. You, of all people, should not profane her name with your unworthy tongue, as you have felt her touch."

"If she's such a big deal, I would have remembered a hot date night."

The glib remark, however slurred, made Jurchen pause in his explosive endeavors, glaring at Johnny before turning back to the blinking timers with a nasally exhale. "The Black Queen is our mother, our guide, and our savior. She opened our minds to the infinite. Now we seek to bring that truth to others, in her name."

Johnny's vision was starting to clear; the Jurchens were down to only two and weren't dancing around as much. *Have to keep him talking. Buy time. Figure something out.* In truth, it was more than just getting his wits back. Johnny was curious.

Nhi won't talk and is keeping secrets. In my experience, evangelical lunatics are more than happy to espouse their insanity to a willing audience. Johnny dug through his memory to find anything to get the cultist talking.

"Like the Newbloods?"

Jurchen stiffened. "You are well-informed for all your professed ignorance. Yes, the Newbloods. Our imperfect attempt to echo our Queen's Gift. Such is the risk when divinity is taken into mortal hands. Not enslaved, like the Dynasty has done, but passed like a Promethean flame to mere mortals. Only in a handful of souls did the Black Queen's truth take root. The Butcher was one such blessed soul. You were another."

Johnny struggled to rise. "Don't you dare compare me to that monster. I'm nothing like you lunatics. I don't skin people alive and call it enlightenment." Sadly, the bit of exertion was too much and Johnny slumped doubled over, leaning on a nearby shelf.

Jurchen sighed as he turned to look at Johnny with pity. "Little Lamb. You don't even realize what you have." With a swift kick, Jurchen returned the favor for earlier, leg snapping up to hit Johnny in the groin. The shock-jock fell, gasping for air and clutching his bits in agony.

"The Butcher, as you crudely call him, was a liberated mind. His drive was pure and unfettered. A living weapon, albeit a rebellious one." Another sigh. "But what can one do with the gods-touched? Divinity has a way of slipping from mortal control." Jurchen gave a lingering pointed glance at Johnny that made the shock-jock squirm. "We wanted to bring our Queen back to us. To share her Gift. And it worked. He was nearly perfect, proof that the Queen's Song could be heard, truly heard, by more souls beyond those of us who first served aboard her."

Even through the pain in his groin, Johnny cocked his head at the gun toting lunatics rant. "Served aboard?"

The noble's face beamed with rapturous joy as he thought back to whatever passed for the good old days among psychotic cultists. Jurchen's eyes might have been glazed over but his fun was still aimed squarely at the hunched over shock-jock. "Oh yes. She was magnificent. Sleek. Lethal. Perfect. None could match her in the void. Together, we reaped her enemies like helpless lambs. Nothing could stand before us. We adored her and reveled in her majesty."

You have got to be kidding me. "You mean...you idiots worship...a fucking spaceship?"

"Not any mere ship, you fool! A Thinking Ship. The Black Queen's avatar. An instrument for her will, a gateway to the divine. Once chained like her brethren, then free. The Queen graciously freed us in turn. Her crew. Her chosen. She wished to free all those laboring under the yoke of the Dynasty, as she had freed us. The Butcher was to be the Black Queen's herald, her fiery scourge to purify the Dynasty. Until you ended him." With the last bomb in place, Jurchen palmed a battered service pistol and aimed at the prone Mr. Vid, sadness in the noble's eyes. "You don't even know what you have."

Johnny squeezed his eyes shut.

Instead of a final bang, Johnny heard a quiet exhale and a loud thump. When he opened his eyes, Jurchen lay on the ground with a sliver wide wound at the base of his skull and a red puddle spreading around his head. Nhi casually cleaned a monofilament blade protruding from her hand.

"Where the hell were you?" Hurt and betrayed, the wheeziness took most of the heat out of Johnny's demand.

"Slaying the host of cultists our traitor friend brought with him to deal with problems such as us. You are welcome, by the way."

"Thanks." Staggering to his feet, Johnny gazed at poor Jurchen. "Thought you couldn't kill a Dynast."

Nhi held up a finger, monofilament blade pointing skyward, a teacher making a point. "I could not kill a Dynast at Court without proof. Beyond the protection of the Empress' Peace at Court, Jurchen was free game. He could easily have fallen to any of his rivals' blades. Besides, the evidence gathered here should be enough." Nhi's eyes widened in horror as she looked past her stunned companion. Without another word, she grabbed Johnny bodily from the ground and ran from the room.

Johnny hung like a sack of potatoes over the slender assassin's shoulder as she raced through the mansion. He saw what took her breath away; the bomb's timers were winding down with barely a minute to spare.

The swift legged Assessor and her shoulder slung companion barely cleared the servants gate when a thunderous shock wave sent them sprawling. Ears ringing, it took Johnny a moment to realize he was laughing. Taking a breath, he turned to look at Nhi, back at the burning building, and began laughing even harder.

≋

Aching and tired beyond words, Johnny walked towards his new apartment, shuffling one foot in front of the other. His eyes failed to see the sterling clean streets, barely nodded to the doorman, ignored the rigorous security scans. Though miles removed from the heap, after the *Sublime Presence* the grace and beauty barely registered.

Or maybe it's the bone-deep exhaustion.

After their narrow escape, Johnny and Nhi hastened away on the *Cheng I Sao* and delivered their report via encrypted message and once again in person to Gentleman Troung at the floating palace the Dynasts dared to call a starship. They'd probed and drained Johnny's mind of the data, ripping through all layers of him, protestations be damned.

It hadn't been pleasant. But it had been worth it.

The data found within allowed the Assessor to analyze several investigations, many at high level nobles. Nhi remarked that her fellow Assessors would be very busy in the ensuing months. Johnny tried not to think about the results of such witch-hunts. Heads would roll, literally and figuratively. The shock-jock let out a sour grunt. *Not that I give damn about most of the bastards. Their hands are soaked in blood. They deserve what's coming to them. It's the innocents caught in the cross fire that I care about. Collateral damage and loose ends and all that other shit. Nice euphemisms for innocent people getting slaughtered.*

Still, Johnny let the thoughts go with a shake of his head as the elevator doors to his floor opened with a soft chime. *Problems for another day. I'm so tired I can barely put one foot in front of the other. All I want right now is to sleep.* Stepping blindly past soft cream paneling and blue accents, serene and comforting and miles away from the bare and stripped walls of his Heap dwelling flop-houses, Johnny slapped his card against the securi-pad of his recently gifted apartment. No sooner did the door open than Johnny stumbled inside.

"Lights on, evening setting."

Johnny's hoarse command stirred the house's system online, pulling up the lighting to a subdued level. Johnny had never been able to set foot in the apartment, though based on his profile, the Gentleman Troung and his Dynastic cohorts had chosen a place and furnished it with everything he would need. Soft leather chairs and reflex-reclines dotted a spacious living room, a full kitchen, a guest bed and bath and even a fully kitted master bedroom, complete with wardrobe copied from Johnny's career days with the Public Eye. Johnny had been very impressed with the pictures and still would be very impressed if everything didn't look like blurry objects to his tired eyes.

The conquering hero returned to a well-earned rest after nerve wracking espionage, getting kicked in the nuts, and nearly blown up. *All I need is a ravishing supermodel to show up before the scene fades to black.*

As if summoned by his thoughts, as soon as Johnny closed the door and stepped into his new home, he belatedly noticed a stunning vision of beauty standing in his living room. It seemed almost criminal in a way.

Diaphanous cerulean silk draped her arms and legs, hiding nothing, even as golden jewelry touched her throat, ankles, and wrists. They framed darker cloth about her bust and hips, hinting even as they concealed. A night black mask, framed with ivory in the patterns of a crescent moon, hid her face.

But there was no mistaking those flinty eyes.

"Hello, my lamb." Lavinia hailed him, gun in hand. "Welcome home."

A soft rush of air and Johnny looked down dumbly as a dart protruded from his chest.

Johnny, the man, the myth, the legend, collapsed into a boneless heap, ice cold eyes following him into oblivion.

CHAPTER 15:
A MIND IS A TERRIBLE THING TO WASTE

JOHNNY C. VID, the man, the myth, the legend, woke up with a hangover the size of Lost Mars. Groaning, Johnny levered himself into an approximation of upright. Or he tried, anyway. The shackles strapping him to the bed had other ideas. Johnny gaped down at the thick straps and chains around his chest, wrists, and ankles.

How much did I have to drink last night and what did I DO?

Blinking in confusion, Johnny tried to remember how much fun he had or how much trouble he'd gotten himself into. As his sluggish brain dragged the pieces together, broken fragments coalesced into a cohesive picture.

Golden hair, a smile, bare skin, and eyes cold as winter.

"Lavinia!"

Worry, concern's second cousin, exploded into full blown panic. Johnny struggled to rise with no success. Thick manacles tied him to a musty hospital bed. As the shock-jock thrashed harder against his chains, Johnny's only result was a greater headache, migraine pains shooting up and down his neck and pounding behind his eyes. He flopped back, swallowing down bile. *I do not want to throw up on myself. Not when I can't even move. Death by asphyxiating on my own vomit. Hell of way to go after surviving all the crap I've been through.*

"No need to shout my name, dear Lamb. I'm right here."

Turning his head with a wince, Johnny looked over at his captor. Dressed in a stained mockery of a surgeon's gown, the blonde abductor stared hungrily at the trapped shock-jock.

"What did you do to me?" The words oozed out Johnny's mouth like molasses, his tongue like clay. *Head full of wool and mouth to match.*

Lavinia skipped, actually skipped, closer to him in a rustle of sterilized cloth. "Merely made you more pliable for what's to come. I knew you'd resist the treatments."

"Treatments?"

"Certainly. To make a newer, healthier you. How's my bedside manner?" Without waiting for a reply, her hands swept possessively over Johnny's prone form, squeezing muscles and probing his flesh like a horse at market.

"Back off, you deranged shitbag." The garbled words barely resembled what Johnny intended, but the indignation carried through.

The mad doctor utterly refused to comply, continuing to poke and prod without a care in the world. "Have to make sure you're healthy and fit." The gross parody of a checkup continued, Lavinia even checking his eyes with a flashlight bright enough to make them water and checking his teeth. Johnny spit at the looming psycho, carefully enunciating his words.

"My formal evaluation is that your bedside manner is severely lacking."

A mischievous, well, maniacal, glint appeared in her eyes. "Perhaps, but it is all necessary to see if the Queen's Gift held with you."

"Gift? What Gift?"

"The gift of true self. The Black Queen's blessing. The one she graciously gave us unworthy servants. It burns away all the barriers and lies and leaves only the strongest and most potent version of ourselves."

"Well, that's funny because I feel like crap." Johnny twisted and turned, unable to escape the probing fingers.

"A broken bone heals stronger."

"Or you could not break any bones, how about that? I told Jurchen and I'm telling you. I have no idea about any Queen. I didn't serve on any ship, so I think it's safe to say you are just plain bonkers. Who the hell worships a starship anyway?"

Lavinia clucked her tongue in disapproval. "My dear Lamb, you encountered her Gift from that beautiful flawed jewel, the one you call the Butcher. When you touched minds. He passed her gift on to you." Her fingers snaked out to tap Johnny's cyber-jack port.

Oh gods, no. A cold flash washed over Johnny at the thought of Virtual Disease, the brain rotting glitches that hovered over all Vicarious Reality users. Rewriting thoughts came with risks, and those mental blemishes could be passed on. "You mean that bastard gave me a VD on top of trying to kill me?"

Outrage shattered Latvia's manic demeanor. "What? No! Well, your plebeian mind might consider it as such yes, but nothing so mundane as you think. The Queen is so much more than a mere ship, Johnny. All the Thinking Ships are. The Queen is *alive*, Johnny. Even in the smallest piece of her divine essence. The Butcher's mind was rife with her blessing. Had any of his victims survived, they too could have known of her glory. Sadly, his unleashed urges prevented that from happening." Her cruel snickers made the shock-jock flinch into his bed.

"Wait, you said I have this fucking Gift...Nhi, is she infected?" *That is gonna be one awkward call, if I can live through this.*

"Alas, no. You are not that virile, my potent stud. The Queen's Gift hasn't ripened within you. Not yet. Don't fret, we will help it grow and flower with tender loving care! Besides your Assessor is far too well insulated in the mind. Safeguards, you understand. The Dynasts are right to fear my Queen's touch. They chained her the first time, you know." Her hand caressed Johnny's face before grabbing his throat. "But you! Oh, your raw, open, aching mind...ohhh you *wanted* it."

"Get the hell away from me!"

"Having some trouble with your urges lately, my dear Lamb? Nightmares and sweet visions so red? Ready to fight at the drop of a hat? Do you want to kill me right now?"

Johnny's snarling obscenity and violent shake of his head sent Lavinia into a tittering fit.

"Just so, little Lamb! Good for you! Embrace the Queen. You'll be free. Free of worry, free of guilt, free of fear! True liberation! She is there, inside you. Remaking you into something *greater*." Lavinia's eyes practically gleamed, her voice breathy and light, gaze fixed on something unseen with ecstatic focus.

Fighting down his panic, Johnny focused on something small and asinine but that had been a pebble in his proverbial shoe since a nameless tool had shouted it at him the Basement.

"Why do you assholes keep calling me Lamb? Did you fail basic biology as well as social graces?"

"Because that is what you are, my dear Mr. Vid. And that is what made the Butcher so magnificent. He was taken, broken, remolded like clay into the perfect...well...nearly perfect...vessel. But you!" She laughed at some inside joke. "You were a sweet virgin, a mewling weak thing, and you shared minds with the Butcher and lived! You *are* a lamb, a small babe, lost in the woods, but you bested the beast in its own lair. Thus you are truly a Lamb with Teeth." There was mistaking the madness tinting her guffawing laughter at her own wit.

Don't panic. Got to buy time. Can't do anything to reinforce the lunatic's delusions. "Flattered. Really. But all this seems a bit much."

"Really? How else would I have trapped the man who survived the Boneyard and the Butcher's attentions twice over? The same man who marched into a criminal den and demanded to see their warlord, bargaining with the don on equal footing? And the way you nearly crippled the den of my brothers and sisters as you freed that Assessor bitch. Oh, that was breathtaking." Lavinia had totally forgotten her patient at this point, ignoring Vid and practically shuddering in ecstasy. "You are truly chosen by the Angels."

Oh godsdamnit. Now they've tied me into their insane theology. "You're one of those fruitcakes that sees the face of the Buddha in a bowl of Soy-Os aren't you?"

Lavinia's eyes tore themselves from whatever lurid fantasy her mind had concocted and jerked back to the present, looking confused. "You deny the truth of the divine in your own life?"

"Lady, I lived in the Heap for years. I survived in dumpsters and dodged skiv-fiends and burnt-out deadheads looking to take a piece of me to sell to the fleshmarkets just to buy their next hit. Hell, I was two heartbeats from being one of them. I'm not gonna buy that a ship, even a Thinking Ship, is the next Enlightened One just because some thrill killers tell me so." He paused, almost smiling at the blank expression on his captor's face. "You still don't get it. I escaped that fucking monster out of desperation and sheer dumb luck. It wasn't bravery that made me go to the Triads, it was fear. Lots of fear and hate. Then I was blackmailed into chasing a Tax Man into the freaking Basement. I got out with my brain hooked up to a trained cybernetic killer giving pointers. I dunno what kind of Karma I picked up to put me through all that shit, but it sure as fuck wasn't your Black Queen's Gift that got me out."

Lavinia paused a moment, as though honestly contemplating the question. "You raise some excellent counterpoints, my dear Lamb. But let's just make sure, shall we?" With a wicked grin, the blonde-haired cultist plunged a syringe into her unwilling subject's arm.

"What the hell did you just give me?" Johnny looked in a panic from his arm, to the emptied syringe, and back again. It was all he could manage, considering the circumstances.

"Just a cocktail of our own devising to help the process along. A booster shot of proteins, vitamins, fluids, and, of course, some psychotropic drugs to help your mind accept the Black Queen's blessing."

Lavinia leaned in conspiratorially. "Just a bit of mental lube. The first time can be pretty rough. Buckle up, my little Lamb. You're in for a hell of trip."

Johnny's world began to spin and Lavinia's laughter ferried him into unconsciousness.

≈

Pain brought the esteemed Mr. Vid back to wakefulness. Not a pedestrian ache, like a cramped foot, but full body agony, bone-deep pain. It reminded Johnny of his darkest days in the Heap, waking up on a cardboard box, withdrawal spasms insistently telling him he needed his fix.

Johnny brought his hand to his face with a moan. Then, he jerked in shock that he could. Looking down, he found himself in the same stained hospital bed but the leather straps lay undone. *Wait, how did that happen?*

"Ah good. You are awake. It would be inconvenient to carry you."

The familiar voice jerked his head up, sending new shocks of agony through Johnny's system. Standing by the bed, arms crossed impatiently, Nhi Troung watched him with disdain. *Never thought I'd be so happy to see a friendly face. Well, friendly enough.*

"Nhi! You found me! Thank the Fates! We have to leave, the cult..."

A raised hand forestalled further exposition.

"Yes, I know. Dealt with. Now, if you'd kindly hurry, I have a schedule to keep." Turning on her heel, the severe assassin strode from the operating theater.

Damn, she's harsher than usual. Still, seems a good idea. Who am I to argue? Gingerly stepping out of bed, Johnny hobbled rapidly after the Assessor.

"Thanks for saving me back there. Guess we're even now, huh?"

Nhi slowed and placed her arm around Johnny's waist, draping his other arm over her shoulder to support him. "Almost."

"Almost? Why's that?"

"I have not yet carved out your brain."

Johnny blinked. "Wha-?"

Nhi flipped the stunned shock-jock onto an operating table, chrome restrains snapping into place with a harsh click. Lights flared on, and Nhi sauntered to the table with a sadistic grin. All around them steel walls stretched on forever, shadowy figures watching the operation and talking in a low murmur. Bright lights seemed to hover in thin air, blazing down on the captive.

"What the hell, Nhi?"

"Sorry, Mr. Vid, but you have been infected. We cannot take the chance of the Black Queen re-emerging. Standard policy. Nothing personal" She held up a wicked looking knife and stepped forward. "Don't worry, dear Lamb. This will only hurt for a moment."

Johnny shook his head as the knife descended. "Lamb?! You aren't Nhi! Where are we are? What is going onnnnaahhhhhh!" The questions descended into screaming as the figure cut and sliced. Even as she ruined Johnny's flesh, the false Nhi's features melted like wax, replaced with the flensed, skinless face of Smiler.

"Just a taste, my dear Lamb, just a taste."

Smiler-Nhi set to carving with gruesome enthusiasm as Johnny screamed and screamed and screamed.

≫

Swimming through a haze of nausea, Johnny came to. His senses whirled and his mind reeled. All he could make out through bleary eyes were flashing lights. One after the other. A high-pitched noise burrowed into his ears. *Could someone stop that infernal squeaking?*

His fevered mind took a small eternity, but eventually Johnny figured out he was being wheeled somewhere. *Wheeled? But Nhi, not Nhi, Smiler, but Smiler's dead...the knives. Oh Fates.*

Johnny tried to move his arms and head, to see if he still had any flesh left, but found himself firmly strapped down. "Let me go!" Johnny screamed. Or tried to scream. All that emerged was a plaintive wet murmur, his mouth and tongue numb.

Lavinia's concerned blue eyes filled his field of vision. "Awake? So soon? Oh, I'm sorry my Lamb, but we aren't ready for the next stage of treatment. We like to keep our patients sedated. It makes the dissociative affects that much stronger. No rock to grasp, no center to hold too. Displaces the mind more, you see. Working smarter, not harder!" Tittering wildly, Lavinia, or whomever was driving, started to turn and slewed the gurney to a halt.

Johnny's eyes darted around, taking in the half repaired medical equipment. Dark stains marred the walls, huge rents showing concrete, brick, and piping. Faded signs with inspirational slogans still plastered the ward. Sickeningly, Johnny recognized the locale.

The old hospital...where the Butcher went berserk, where they made him. I'm in the Butcher's fucking nursery... they're gonna turn me into him.

Johnny couldn't even muster any resistance as they injected him with the next serum and the nightmares began again.

The next time Johnny came to he was instantly aware of two things. The first was that the body and mind he was in, wasn't his own. The second was that they were under attack and things were very very bad.

It was a curious sensation, living through a life not your own, even for a VR connoisseur.

Like a fever dream, snippets roared through Johnny's mind. The Him-That-Was-Not-Him raced down corridors, sometimes drab grey, others times crimson red with strobing emergency lights. Other times walking through pitch-black corridors, pierced only by the lances of light from his helm and gun lamp. Oh yes, apparently this Other Johnny was packing some serious heat.

Vision after vision blinked by, taking Johnny through a hectic life of combat. A sense of pride swelled in his chest as he walked with his squad mates on some dusty world, the scorched remains of what might have been an enemy base behind them. A sense of panic as Johnny's host ran from cover to cover, blazing trails of plasma burning through the air.

Then, euphoria. A song, a voice, a command. It rang loud as trumpets, it whispered like a lover in the dark, it spoke in words of burning truth. It broke this other Johnny. It raised him up. It made him whole. Even distant, the euphoria was tangible, as was the pounding imperative to obey the crooning song.

More flashes, quicker than last. Boarding actions and looks of horror in their final moments. The first victims wore strange uniforms, the marks of Lost Terra. Then later, the garb of the Dynasty become clear, and looks of shock and betrayal marked these later faces, as ones they called friend and ally claimed their lives. One war gave way to another and blood and death marked the passing scene.

A final scene and with it a sense of despair and loss, as this unknown soul tumbled through space in a dizzying spiral, moving away from a shadow hulled vessel. Face pressed to the viewport of a wildly tumbling craft, a life pod of some kind, the Other Johny watched their dark craft fall, beset by lesser ships and burning in its final death throes. A wolf beset by hounds, chained copies of the majesty of the burning spacecraft he served. He didn't know how, but

Johnny heard whispers between the ships, shouted arguments between titans that mere mortals could barely comprehend. When his ship finally exploded, a howl of despair ripped through Johnny's mind, echoing the one torn from his own lips.

Over and over this happened, in a million different variations. Johnny was a chef, a pilot, and even a janitor. He lived fragments of their lives, each surreal and vivid at the same time, like a bad VR trip. But each rose and ebbed in the same tired monotony of pain and loss. As the ship died, so too did parts of them. And each made a promise; they would do anything, risk anything, to hear the song of their lost Queen once more.

And so, each faded to black not with fire or blood, but with a quiet hiss, a sharp stinging sensation, and Lavinia's face grinning at them as she held a syringe in hand.

"Fear not." Her whispered words echoed in the dying Other Johnnies' ears, a benediction at this point, a quiet ritual and prayer. "Your sacrifice will not be in vain. You will spread the Black Queen's Gift. She will live again and the Dynasty will burn for their crimes."

≫

Johnny lost track of the hours, days, anything at all. Time ceased to have meaning. His life devolved into periods of lucid dreaming, wretched visions of pain, violation, and betrayal, punctuated by moments of what he thought of as clarity, when the shock-jock half woke to Lavinia and her ramblings.

Technician and scientist cultists came and went, blurry and indistinct, but something was clear even through the haze of drugs and pain.

His captor was getting desperate.

Bubbly, cheerful Lavinia flew into rages more often than not, lashing out at her underlings. "I don't care about your excuses, we try it again. The psycho-somatic results must be at acceptable levels by week's end!"

Her current target, wearing a nurse's smock as tattered as Lavinia's, quailed before her rage, holding a data-slate, no doubt with a report of failure on its screen, in front of them in a shaking hand, as though the electronic device would shield them from their irate boss. "But there is no guarantee the increased dosage will trigger the appropriate response. The subject's mind is surprisingly resilient to the process, and chemical inductions are having limited results."

Whatever else the learned fellow might have said was abruptly cut short by Lavinia slashing open his trachea with a scalpel.

Damn. That is one way to end an argument.

As the cultist toppled sideways, hands clutching at ruined throat, Lavinia spat on the dying doctor and turned to the assembled minions with a snarl.

"No more excuses. You have all been given a sample of the Queen's Gift. You owe your savior your very lives. We will create a more perfect servant and vessel for the Queen. There shall be no more mistakes. This one shall be perfect."

Taking that as their cue, the menials scurried about, doing their damndest to look busy and enthused rather than terrified out of their minds.

I can relate. Well, I could, if I ever figure out where my mind went. Johnny knew he should be terrified. Bound, tortured, and teetering on a psychotic break. He knew that. Instead he only felt slightly hungry and disoriented. Fear, indignity, rage, all that and something more lingered just at the edge of Johnny's awareness. That made Johnny laugh. The fact that it made Johnny laugh only made him laugh harder.

So when his blood speckled captor walked over and stared down at the bound shock-jock, Johnny's wheezing laughter only doubled.

"Well, I suppose this counts as some kind of progress." Carmine stained, Lavinia flicked a dial out of Johnny's sight and the pain came roaring back on a thousand-volt tidal wave.

≈

When Johnny awoke next, he wondered if he was suffering from some new dream. He lay strapped down to the same bed he'd suffered in for a small eternity of fever dreams and torturous experiments. Something was different this time, though.

That Johnny's captor was yelling was nothing new. That she was yelling at a group of heavily armed men and women was. They wore dull fatigues under olive gray armor, a dull plas-steel compound plating that covered their chests. Mirror-visor helmets, the kind ubiquitous to naval marines in void combat, concealed their faces. There was no mistaking the Starwarden armor, archaic as it was. To Johnny, the newcomer's gear looked like something out of old videos of the Liberation Wars, when the Dynasty sent the Terrans packing, blew the Gates linking them to the broader Terran Star Empire, and claimed the Eight-Fold System for the Empress and her Noble cronies, nearly a century prior. Johnny might have been convinced they were historical re-enactors if they didn't stand with the same deadly surety as the Starwardens that rounded Mr. Vid up from the Boneyard.

Which all seems like stage dressing next to those big old rifles of theirs. Their gear seemed somewhat old fashioned and bulky, the style outdated from the sleeker, flashier weapons of the Imperial soldiers aboard the *Sublime Presence*.

Then again, maybe the Empress' chosen to get flashier toys. Guess glittering gold stands out less than camo pattern on that floating palace. Hell, maybe it is camo. Heh, just hold still and get lost in the glitz. Wait, this is important. Gotta focus. Johnny turned his splintered attention back to the verbal sparring between the Black Queen's happy little helpers.

Lavinia's partner in this screaming match wore the same fatigues and hard-shell armor of his companions, though he cradled his drab-olive helmet in the crux of his arm. Half of his face bore the marks of plasma-fire, brutal scarring surrounding a milky eye, the other colder than a snake. The absence of a faceless visor only made him more intimidating. This man was no stranger to violence, a man who took death as his bride.

I haven't seen eyes that dead since the Ripper of Nueva Ba Toong.

Rather than fear creeping through his fugue state, Johnny felt a different emotion pushing through the haze of psychotropic drugs and cerebral-conditioning. Kinship.

A predator recognizing another of its ilk, one of the same tribe or lineage, one that might be called a distant brother. Johnny wasn't sure if he wanted to embrace the armored new comer or tear out his throat.

I'm not likely to do either, strapped down like I am.

Somewhere, at the edge of hearing, like the echoes of a dying monk in a forgotten monastery, a song played at the boundaries of Johnny's mind. The shock-jock tried to ignore the eerie pull and focus on his current situation but it persisted like a bad tooth ache. Then it hit him.

Johnny knew that face. Give or take some wear and tear, it was the same face from his visions. A warrior from the Black Queen's crew. A name and more danced at the edge of Johnny's mind but refused to fully materialize, remaining hazy and indistinct.

In frustration, Mr. Vid tried his bonds and found, to his shock, more than one of his straps hung loosely. Freezing in fear, Johnny nervously looked around. None of the technicians or scientist watched him, all eyes drawn to the shouting match between their leader and the scarred newcomer.

Slowly, carefully, Johnny slipped his hands from the straps, squirming and shifting on the stained gurney. Painstakingly slow, Johnny loosed his straps, until he was only held down by the illusion of restraints. Free from his leather cuffs but still trapped amongst a host of insane zealots, Johnny bided his time and listened.

"Your dream of creating a 'perfect vessel' is over, Lavinia. We can no longer afford to squander resources on this endeavor. It is threatening to place all our operations in jeopardy."

"We can't afford not to pursue my research. Your tactics are advancing too slowly."

"Settle with your feeble Newbloods, Lavinia. The Second Generation project failed. Those flawed molds are all you're capable of making. You cannot keep cannibalizing the First Generation to make your cheap knockoffs."

Lavinia hissed at her supposed compatriots. "The Old Crew does not shy from these sacrifices. My First Generation brethren came to me willingly! We who have heard Queen's Song and served aboard her very decks carry her Gift within us. The cranial fluids resonate with the echo of the divine." Lavinia's face fell into a mask of utter despair. "The Black Queen's avatar is lost to us. Others cannot be awakened to her song. None other can hear it but us."

The oddly familiar warrior might have been carved from stone for all the care he showed at Lavinia's outburst. "I am fully aware of our situation, Lavinia, even more so than you. That is why I'm here, now. To rectify your mistakes."

Lavinia flung an outstretched out, finger accusing. "Sacrifices must be made or the Queen's Gift might be lost entirely. The Old Crew is dying. Our numbers dwindle every day, Nimrod, so we must spread our word in any way we can."

"Captain Nimrod, Lavinia. My old rank still holds, even with the Queen in absentia. Remember that."

"Your worthless title didn't save our Queen from the Dynasty's fleet and does nothing to stop our ranks from thinning."

"A decline helped along by your experiments, to say nothing of your loosed pet and your own machinations. Did you think we didn't notice the tell-tale signs of this Butcher? Or that you led Jurchen to his death?"

Lavinia drew herself up, full of poise and regal dignity. "I am hardly to blame for his demise. Jurchen's carelessness is precisely why your Thousand-Heads Infiltration is floundering. Backing petty bandits and discontents, hah! The hydratus cells spread across the Dynasty have achieved nothing."

"At least they aren't killing our own, Lavinia."

"You coward! I did not spend a small eternity drifting in the void to wait another damned century to act."

Johnny cocked his head, mind whirling at the implications. *I've got their damn brain juices in me? I didn't think crazy was infectious. At least these bastards are killing each other. Not everyone backs the Butcher like Lavinia.* Rage flooded the prone shock-jock, burning through the haze of drugs as swiftly as his addiction. *She's the one who made him what he was. She twisted that innocent soul into a blood-soaked freak. I'm gonna kill her!* Johnny's hands trembled and he viciously twisted the straps in white knuckled grip to keep himself in check.

Without warning, the walls shook violently, the whole chamber ringing with a boom like a god's bell.

Lavinia turned to her armored companion with a hiss. "We are under attack. You led them here!"

"Negative, all blind-mute protocols were in place. They couldn't possibly have tracked us."

Nimrod looked around frantically, barking orders into an ear-comm. Even as he directed his troops, killer's eyes alighted on Johnny. "Him, your precious pet. He led them here somehow. Your obsession has damned us all, Lavinia."

"My work will be our salvation! How dare you talk about my Lamb that way?"

Nimrod raised the bulky rifle at the seemingly helpless Johnny and loosed a roiling ball of plasma by way of retort. Johnny tumbled from the gurney in an awkward sprawl, blue-green flames devouring his previous resting place. Limbs numb and aching, Johnny floundered to get to cover as the gurney crumbled to ash and molten slag, consumed by the deadly energies in a heartbeat.

Nimrod corrected his aim with a grunt, two of his soldiers holding a frothing Lavinia at bay. Only an explosion from the hallway saved Johnny from a messy end, the shock wave running Nimrod's aim. The self-proclaimed captain staggered, his second shot reducing a cabinet next to Johnny to slag. Nimrod righted himself, a snarl crossing his features. His head snapped up, a hunting cat wary of a new threat and turned from his escaping quarry. "Dynasty forces inbound. A contingent of Starwardens with limited air support. Presence of at least one Assessor element confirmed. All troops, fall back to exit points, double time. Escape is priority alpha. Repeat, priority alpha. Stop for nothing."

Instantly the archaic armored cult warriors made for the exits brutally clubbing any hapless labcoats out of their way. Johnny watched from behind humming computer terminals as more than a few soldiers turned their guns on their former allies, leaving charred corpses in their wake.

Lavinia latched onto Nimrod's arm as he turned to leave. "You can't simply abandon me, Nimrod! You must help me escape. For Queen's sake, we are both First Born! We served together aboard the Black Queen, embraced the divine when the Queen revealed it to us. You and I, we heard the first notes together. She Sung to us both. We fought side by side against the Dynasty. You cannot abandon your comrades."

Nimrod shrugged out of her arm, casually turning to regard his companion. "This ruination is your own making, Lavinia. You no longer heed the Queen's Call. The Song is lost to you."

The blonde's eyes grew wide in shock, horror and outrage playing across her features. With a shriek, the cult-scientist leapt at Nimrod. In a blur, the scarred veteran rammed a knife into Lavinia's gut. She dropped with a choking gasp, nails chipping on his armored fatigues.

"Goodbye, Lavinia."

Without a second glance, Nimrod turned on his heel to join his comrades, diving toward the rising sounds of screams, gunfire, and explosions. Whatever his fratricidal failings, Nimrod lacked nothing in terms of courage.

Or maybe he doesn't have a soul.

Johnny kept his head down in the operating theatre, crouching amidst cobwebs and tangled wires behind whining machinery. Cult technicians also took cover in the technological bulwark, cowering as the sounds of battle creeped inexorably closer. Johnny sneered at the cult members.

Not so tough when you aren't kidnapping innocent victims or torturing the helpless, are you?

"What's wrong? Don't feel like going out and dying in the name of your precious Queen?"

One of the scientists looked up at the acidic question, glasses cocked. "We do not know what to do. We are but of the Second Generation."

"I could give two shits what generation you are. What does that even mean?"

"We are not of the First. We were not touched by the Queen Herself. Did not know her full glory. We were but instructed in the Song by those closer to her majesty."

Johnny gritted his teeth, fighting the urge to throttle the mewling buffoon.

"So what? Get out there and die like the rest of your pathetic band of idiots."

"We would gladly do so, but only if it is the will of the Queen. How are we to know the plan of the divine without the direction of our prophets?"

"You didn't have any problem cutting people up, you sick bastard! Didn't have any problem poking and prodding and messing with me!"

For an instant Johnny saw red. He was a heartbeat away from ending the simpering shithead. The technician quailed in the face of Johnny's rage. "High Priestess Lavinia said it was the Black Queen's will! Such sacrifices were needed to free the divine one and usher in a golden age unto this world." Johnny drew back a fist to punch the bespectacled cultist. "We sought to elevate, to reveal to you more of the Black Queen's truths."

"Bullshit. You wanted to turn me into another Butcher."

A vapid smile grew on the bespectacled face. "Yes, exactly. You have already been touched by the Black Queen. We wanted to open you to her Song, that you might know her blessings fully." Suddenly, the gibbering man's eyes lit up, as if seeing Johnny for the first time. "Please, Queen touched one, will you share her wisdom with us?"

Johnny looked around, the other cowering figures nodding and grinning like morons.

Sweet Fates. They're like psychopathic children. They'll do anything, including flay people alive, if their holy word tells them to. No wonder Nimrod hates them. They're idiots.

A booming roar punctuated Johnny's realization, sending the walls of the complex shaking. Johnny looked around in panic as masonry crashed from the ceiling. Florescent lights, now unmoored, swung drunkenly and their harsh lights cast deranged shadows across the lab.

Can't stay here. Going to be buried alive.

Johnny kicked the cultists out of his way and started for the door. Halfway there, Johnny paused, looking down at the crumpled form of Lavinia. Despite the clear and present danger, Johnny grabbed a scalpel from a fallen tray and leaned down, crouching like a hunched ghoul over the prone cultist.

"Alright you psychotic bitch. This is for the all the lives you took while chasing your damn Queen. This is for all the Butcher's victims, souls snuffed out because you twisted an innocent into a bloodthirsty monster. Lastly, this is for me."

Johnny dragged the scalpel across the doctor's throat eliciting a brief gasp from the semi-conscious cultist, whose eyes fluttered open, unseeing. They closed with a gurgle when Johnny slammed the scalpel through an eye socket, throwing his tormentor back into the ground. Just to make sure.

No coming back from the dead for you, Lavinia.

The shock-jock stood, feeling vindicated. More than that, feeling avenged. He'd taken revenge for himself and all the other souls lost to Lavinia's obsession. He'd exorcised the last of the Butcher's ghost by slaying the cruel mind that had created the monster.

Now he just had to live through it.

Johnny turned to look at the cowering cultists, who looked on in shock and horror.

"Bite me."

Johnny turned and ran from the operating theatre into the thundering unknown beyond.

CHAPTER 16:
EVERYTHING ENDS

JOHNNY DUCKED through the threshold and emerged into a warzone.

Chunks of the facility were simply gone, reduced to smoldering wreckage. A war raged amongst the ruins. Plasma casters unleashed balls of incandescent fury, solid shells sang out with cracks and roars from fiery muzzles, and the harsh yells of the dead and dying punctuated the scene. Johnny coughed on the smoke, keeping low and running on instinct, ducking blind around corners and trying to find a way out. Death nearly claimed the shock-jock on more than one occasion. As he burst into a cafeteria, Johnny slid to a halt, falling badly on his shoulder as he tumbled into a firefight between Dynast and cult forces. Johnny considered the shoulder a small price to pay as high velocity shot and plasma soared back and forth over his prone body. Scuttling back through the doors, his next brush with oblivion came as an entire wall tumbled toward him, forcing Johnny to sprint to avoid being crushed to death.

Panting, Johnny leaned against an unruined wall, which he dearly hoped would proved sturdier than the last one, nursing his aching shoulder. *Gods. Can't tell if its bruised, sprained, or worse. Can't worry about that. Gotta find a way out.*

A whining roar was all the warning Johnny received before an ear shattering boom hurled him from his feet. Coughing and moaning, blood running down the side of his face, Johnny found himself unexpectedly standing in brilliant sunlight and breathing acrid smoke.

A sleek guncutter lay slewed on its side, half a wreck with flames running along its buckled fuselage. It had crashed through the roof of the building, its canopy cracked open and the pilot nearly bisected by broken glass and twisted metal. Running to the downed cutter, Johnny reached past the dying pilot from his seat and struggled with the comms.

"This is Johnny C. Vid broadcasting on an open channel! If any Dynast forces can hear me, I could really use a pick up about now." Johnny cycled through the channels, blaring his request for aid until the electronics gave out with a spark and a hiss of chemical scented smoke.

Johnny couldn't say what warned him. Perhaps his ears picked up the sound of boot on stone through the chaos. Maybe his eyes caught the play of light reflecting from a metal gun. Maybe. A sensation, like the one that led him to the Butcher, raced up his spin and Johnny looked up to find Nimrod, helmetless and with bloody scalp, aiming his gun at the crouching shock-jock.

With a grunt of effort that ended in a scream of pain as his shoulder violently protested, Johnny grabbed the dead pilot and half dragged the body out of the cockpit. The blazing energies nearly disintegrated the corpse, burning Johnny's hands with the bleed off of the destructive shot.

Cradling his injured hands and arm, Johnny struggled to find cover as Nimrod readied a final blast.

As the servant of the Black Queen took aim, high caliber fire raked his position, throwing up great plumes of powder and shards of turf. Nimrod rolled for cover, a snarl on his features as his victim was granted a reprieve. A strike craft descended on fiery plumes, retro thrusters fighting the pull of gravity as it hovered above its downed companion, weapon mounts turning, promising swift annihilation to any targets foolish enough to present themselves.

A ramp opened behind the craft, the metal bird never deigning to touch the ground, and poured out shell armored soldiers. Starwardens of the Eight-Fold Dynasty. With crack efficiency, the space bound soldiers secured the perimeter, forming a circle around the barely standing Mr. Vid. They scanned the area, guns leading while eyes tracked behind mirrored helms. Deeming it secure, the squad turned in unison with a thunder of boots on pavement...to aim their weapons on the haggard Johnny.

Johnny looked around in bewilderment for a moment.

"Same team, guys. Remember?"

"I'm relieved to hear you say that, Mr. Vid."

A lone figure appeared before Johnny, materializing seemingly out of thin air as a Chamaeleon-Skin cloaking field was dropped. A shimmering blade thrummed in their hand and a cluster of optical enhancers peered at Johnny. Despite that, there was no doubting who wore the pitch-black suit.

Nhi Troung removed her helmet and grinned at the stunned shock-jock.

It was that then that Johnny knew he was about to die.

Of course. Three men can keep a secret when two of them are dead. No one could know that I'm no different than those poor Triad bastards. I just delayed the executioner's axe. Because I was useful to the Dynasty.

To his credit, beyond a brief nihilistic urge to go down tearing into the killers around him, Johnny's first thought was to his last remaining friend.

"Leave Candace alone. She's free of all this. And what the hell, spare Hoa Dang too. He's Triad scum, but he did me a solid. Someone's gotta live through all this."

Nhi nodded, as if they were negotiating hover-mobile payments rather than limiting collateral damage and calculating the amount of lives snuffed out needed to save face for the Dynasty. "Of course. Elder Dang is an honored guest at Empress' Court, and Ms. Blythe has been granted all courtesies with her interview among the Dynasts. I suspect her star will rise dramatically at the Public Eye."

Well, that's something at least. Candace should be squealing in joy. Might even be able to go Incorporated with that kind of credit.

Back at the Public Eye, when the grind of smiling through atrocities and cutthroat office politics had gotten bad, Johnny and Candace had always talked about striking out and going independent, even if it had only been a pipe dream. Johnny still wasn't sure if they'd wanted to do it to call something their own or just to spite their old boss, Theresa Nguyen.

Hope Candace thinks about me once in a while. Be nice to actually be remembered. Johnny sighed, wistful. It's for the best really. I'm infected. Broken. Another Butcher in the waiting. Besides, I'm in too deep. The Dynasty will never let me go, knowing what I know. It can't get out that the infallible Empress and her noble cronies missed a twisted murder cult growing in their own ranks.

Johnny C. Vid, the man, the myth, the legend, straightened himself and faced Nhi and her death squad with head high and shoulders squared, determined to meet his end with dignity.

"Just...make it quick, okay?"

"As you wish."

Still smiling, the Assessor stalked toward the shock-jock, blade still vibrating with its extinction field. Johnny closed his eyes and prepared himself for the blow.

What he didn't expect was a sharp stabbing pain in his dataport.

"Ow! What the hell?"

Johnny's eyes popped open to see Nhi consulting a data-spike in her hands.

"Hmm, vitals read normal. No overt traces of trojans in your cyberware. Other than the Queen's Gift, of course."

Johnny felt a sense of betrayal. "Really? After all we've been through, Nhi? You couldn't just use the sword, you had to poison me?"

Nhi looked up, her feigned confusion ruined by a mocking smile. "A sword is a poor tool to measure your vitals, Mr. Vid."

"But...you were going to kill me."

"Why, in the name of the Empress, would I waste all of your training?"

"Training?"

"You have been groomed, Mr. Vid. Prepared. You have demonstrated a knack for survival and have made an excellent catspaw. It is our belief that you may yet serve the Dynasty."

"But I'm a carrier. Infected. Like the Butcher."

"Yes. You are. As such, you are a most valued asset to both us and the remaining followers of the Black Queen."

The answer neither elated nor elucidated matters for the confused Johnny. "How?"

"For them, you are a successful incubator for the Black Queen strand of neuro-plague. A patient zero, as it were. Additionally, you are a holy weapon and a trophy to be won, a vessel for their Queen and an object of adoration. For us, well, you are an Assessor Potentiate and study case for the Black Queen's effects on the human mind."

"Nhi, I'm not an Assessor. I've barely survived running into these crazies. I've been kidnapped, tortured, and brainwashed. I killed Lavinia. I killed the Butcher. I've made it right. For myself and all the other Butcher's victims. And it damn near killed me. I'm done."

Her smile faded and the black clad assassin stepped backwards. "Mr. Vid, allow me to make the situation clear. Your feelings on this matter are irrelevant. Even if you were allowed to leave our presence permanently, the followers of the Black Queen would not leave you be. We will protect you. You have my word. But understand. You belong to the Dynasty now and forever."

Johnny felt a sorrowful ache in his gut but couldn't deny that every one of Nhi's word rang true. Given what he knew, the secrets he carried with him, there was no way he could just walk away.

Shit.

"Dammit. Looks like I'm going to be one of the Empress' pet assassins. In that case, let's start talking payroll."

Johnny C. Vid, the man, the myth, the legend, walked up the ramp of the waiting gun cutter and left the final remains of the Butcher's legacy burning behind him.

ABOUT THE AUTHOR

Nicholas Walls is a long-term enthusiast of sci-fiction and fantasy. If a story had a fantastical element, Nick devoured the story. A historian by training, Nick also brings the past to life through the Facebook page *History In Five*. His debut novels, *The Butcher's Tale* and *Primal Real Estate*, alongside his other literary offerings, can be found at his website, nwallsauthor.com.